Tanner Picked Up The Ring— An Exquisite Cluster Of Yellow Diamonds Set In Platinum— And Held It Out. "May I?"

He took Abby's hand in his and slipped the ring on her finger.

What now? What was she supposed to say now, as his gaze blazed down into hers, gold fire and pure heat?

Somewhere a bell chimed. A soft, tinkling sound that barely nudged her from her dreamlike state.

He smiled knowingly. "Are you ready, *Mrs*. Tanner...?"

Her stomach flipped over at the intimate, husky sound of his voice. Soft, low, caressing...

She was falling hard and fast for this charade.

She needed to remember that Cinderella turned back into a poor servant girl at midnight—or in this case at the end of the weekend—and that the looks "Prince Charming" was giving her were only part of his act....

* * *

"Who could ask for more?
Romance, chocolate and a wonderful new voice
in Silhouette Desire. You're going to love
Cinderella & the Playboy. It's one sweet deal."
—*New York Times* bestselling author
Debbie Macomber

Dear Reader,

What could be more satisfying than the sinful yet guilt-free pleasure of enjoying six new passionate, powerful and provocative Silhouette Desire romances this month?

Get started with *In Blackhawk's Bed*, July's MAN OF THE MONTH and the latest title in the SECRETS! miniseries by Barbara McCauley. *The Royal & the Runaway Bride* by Kathryn Jensen—in which the heroine masquerades as a horse trainer and becomes a princess—is the seventh exciting installment in DYNASTIES: THE CONNELLYS, about an American family that discovers its royal roots.

A single mom melts the steely defenses of a brooding ranch hand in *Cowboy's Special Woman* by Sara Orwig, while a detective with a secret falls for an innocent beauty in *The Secret Millionaire* by Ryanne Corey. A CEO persuades a mail-room employee to be his temporary wife in the debut novel *Cinderella & the Playboy* by Laura Wright, praised by *New York Times* bestselling author Debbie Macomber as "a wonderful new voice in Silhouette Desire." And in *Zane: The Wild One* by Bronwyn Jameson, the mayor's daughter turns up the heat on the small town's bad boy made good.

So pamper the romantic in you by reading all six of these great new love stories from Silhouette Desire!

Enjoy!

Joan Marlow Golan

Joan Marlow Golan
Senior Editor, Silhouette Desire

Please address questions and book requests to:
Silhouette Reader Service
U.S.: 3010 Walden Ave., P.O. Box 1325, Buffalo, NY 14269
Canadian: P.O. Box 609, Fort Erie, Ont. L2A 5X3

Cinderella &
the Playboy
LAURA WRIGHT

Published by Silhouette Books
America's Publisher of Contemporary Romance

First, I thank God
With His hand on my shoulder, anything is possible....

This book is dedicated to two amazing people: my husband,
Daniel Ionazzi, and my best friend and critique partner, Julie Hogan.
Where one gave me wings to fly headfirst into my dream, the other
gave me fresh air and clear skies. You are the rocks, the ears and the
encouraging voice. I love you both with all of my heart.

 SILHOUETTE BOOKS

ISBN 0-373-76451-0

CINDERELLA & THE PLAYBOY

Copyright © 2002 by Laura Wright

LAURA WRIGHT

has spent most of her life immersed in the world of acting, singing and competitive ballroom dancing. But when she started writing romance, she knew she'd found the true desire of her heart! Although born and raised in Minneapolis, Minnesota, Laura has also lived in New York, Milwaukee and Columbus, Ohio. Currently she is happy to have set down her bags and made Los Angeles her home. And a blissful home it is—one that she shares with her theatrical production manager husband, Daniel, and three spoiled dogs. On those few hours of downtime from her beloved writing, Laura enjoys going to art galleries and movies, cooking for her hubby, walking in the woods, lazing around lakes, puttering in the kitchen and frolicking with her animals. Laura would love to hear from you. You can e-mail her at laurawright@laurawright.com.

Acknowledgments

To my teacher, mentor and friend, Barbara Ankrum:
I'm forever in your debt
for showing me this exquisite world.

To my best girls,
Julie Ganis, Tami Goveia and Patti Chung:
I thank you so much for your friendship
and hard work, and I share this with you.

To my Aunt Marsha: Thank you for being you....

A special thanks to Steve Philipson
for teaching me all about gliders and soaring in them
(from the ground, of course).

And to you who are reading this: May I always grant you
words from my heart and stories from my soul.

One

"**Y**ou need a wife."

It was a ridiculous piece of advice and C. K. Tanner barely raised an eyebrow before responding, "You're fired."

"You can't fire me." Jeff Rhodes grinned widely. "I'm too valuable…your CFO *and* your friend." He slid a fax across Tanner's massive desk. "And speaking as both, I see no other way. Two other corporations are chomping at the bit for this deal, and both CEOs have wives. It looks to me like Frank Swanson wants an honest, good old-fashioned family man. So if you're hell-bent on acquiring the Swanson Sweets Candy Company, you'd better consider producing a Mrs. Tanner ASAP."

Swiveling around in his chair, Tanner turned to face the floor-to-ceiling windows. From his offices on the thirty-first floor, he stared out across the city of Los Angeles and beyond to the ocean. It was a crystal-clear Wednesday in October—no smog, perfect sunshine— but he barely saw it. His mind raced to find another solution to the problems plaguing what should have been an easy purchase. He wanted that candy company. Hell, he wanted every company that posed a challenge to him. Acquisitions seemed to fill a hole in him, even if the feeling was only temporary.

Jeff was right, though. Acquiring Swanson Sweets was going to take more than quick thinking, clever strategies and Tanner's trademark never-say-die negotiating style.

Friday morning he was flying to Minneapolis. He was the last of the competitors to stay with the Swansons for the weekend. It was a chance for each man to see how the company was run, tour the plant, and get to know the family behind the chocolate.

"I spoke with Harrison this morning," Jeff said, breaking off Tanner's thoughts.

Tanner inhaled sharply. Mitchell Harrison was as ruthless a businessman as they came. He also wanted to own Swanson Sweets—and would be willing to pay top dollar for the honor. Harrison's own candy company was a longtime rival to Swanson Sweets, and he was looking to eliminate the competition. But the man was three times divorced and a notorious womanizer. Tanner had heard through the acquisition grapevine that Swanson wouldn't even review a bid from Harrison—no matter how high he went. And Tanner couldn't help but assume that the reason was rooted in Harrison's spotty reputation.

Jeff cleared his throat. "He's willing to pay a hefty premium to buy Swanson Sweets from you once you get it from Swanson."

"I'm still considering it," Tanner answered tightly.

Tanner ground his teeth. What the hell was he considering anyway? Buying and selling. It was his standard M.O. But in this case, taking a man's life's work and selling it to the highest bidder—to someone who only wanted to dissolve the company—well, for some reason this time that wasn't sitting very well with him.

For forty-two years, Frank Swanson had poured everything he had into his candy company, built it from the ground up, with his family by his side. He was ready to retire and had two married daughters who weren't interested in taking over. He was willing to sell, but his actions seemed to verify Jeff's assumption that Swanson would only sell to someone with values similar to his own.

Tanner rubbed his jaw. Why any man would choose to settle down, get married and have children was beyond him. All investment and no return. Perhaps if you could see into someone's heart, know their motivations, predict their actions, it might work. But you couldn't. Family was trouble with a capital *T*.

He had little room for opinions in this matter. If a wife was what it was going to take to win, Tanner would sure as hell do it.

He leaned back in his chair. "So the question now becomes who."

"How about Olivia?" Jeff prompted.

"I don't think so."

"Karen?"

"Too aggressive."

"What about that actress you were seeing?"

Tanner chuckled and stood up. "And have every conversation reduced to liposuction and fat grams?" He walked over to the bar and poured himself a glass of water. "This woman can't be anyone I see socially, Jeff. I don't want my female friends thinking marriage is ever an option with me. I need a simple woman, sweet, elegantly dressed. Educated, but not snobbish. No party girls."

Jeff muttered an oath. "This *is* L.A. Where are you going to look? The library?"

Tanner drained his glass. "Why not? I can turn a sparrow into a swan if I have to."

Jeff laughed. "Hell, if you're looking for a sparrow, why not try your mail room?"

Tanner's head came up with a snap. "What's in the mail room?"

"My secretary informs me that the hardworking ladies down there run a sort of daily Tanner Watch. Most of them have quite a crush, apparently." With a snort, he added, "Well, all except for one, she says."

Tanner sat down on the edge of his desk, fascinated by Jeff's knowledge of the downstairs machinations of Tanner Enterprises. "Oh, really? And who does your secretary say that one is?"

"Abby something-or-other." Jeff chuckled.

A redhead with killer green eyes and a soft mouth snaked through Tanner's mind. Polite and shy, the pretty lady who brought him his mail never tried to catch his eye like most of the women in the office. She wore frumpy, conservative clothes to hide whatever she felt she had to hide, but Tanner had always had a sneaking suspicion that what she was hiding was worth a look.

But he'd never know. The woman had a demeanor—a look he could spot with accuracy—that had "home and hearth" written all over it. And he stayed a million miles away from women like that.

"You know," Jeff began, a light glowing in his eyes that made Tanner nervous. "She'd be perfect, boss."

"Perfect for what?"

"To play the role of your wife. I hear she's sweet and simple and smart. And she's definitely not someone you see socially." Jeff's grin widened. "There's also no chance of her wanting more from you because, hey, according to the office scuttle, she doesn't like you at all." He chuckled. "Hot damn, I never thought I'd see the day when a woman could resist the great C. K. Tanner. I think I might be in love with this girl myself!"

A scowl found its way to Tanner's face. "I'll tell you what, Jeff. How about if I give you two minutes to get back to work before I fire you?"

Jeff laughed, stood up and headed for the door. "All right, all right. It was just a thought. I guess you don't need my help if you're going on a wife hunt, anyway. You've always done just fine with the ladies on your own."

"Damn right I have," Tanner muttered as the door closed. But still, the idea lingered.

He leaned back in his chair. How about enlisting a woman who didn't like him? No strings, no calls afterward. Strictly business. That would make things pretty neat and tidy when it was time for a "divorce," wouldn't it?

His gaze flickered to the Swanson file that lay open on his desk. Challenges made a great life even better. If his first challenge was to persuade the head of Swanson Sweets to sell him his company, why not enlist the help of the second challenge to do it?

With a satisfied, confident smile, Tanner flipped through the file as he awaited the arrival of his daily mail with grossly uncharacteristic anticipation.

Funky Latin music reverberated off the cold, white walls in the mail room of Tanner Enterprises. Abby McGrady salsa'd her cart, piled high with packages and letters, toward the elevator, grazing the edges of a few desks on her way, mumbling a "sorry" to the chipped paint.

"Say hi to my boyfriend," Dixie Watts called from the sorting area. "Let Mr. Tanner know that he can pick me up on the loading docks at seven for our date."

Balancing several cups of coffee on a tray as she walked past Abby, Janice Miggs put in her two cents. "And since he changes women every week, tell him I'm available next Friday."

"Every week?" Mary Larson laughed. "Try every hour on the hour." Then she waved over at Abby.

"That certainly doesn't mean I'm not free next hour or the hour after that."

"Stop teasing her," Alice Balton said. "You know how she feels about him."

Dixie raised an amused brow. "And she knows how *we* feel about him."

Laughter filled the large, windowless room. Several of the girls hooted and catcalled, while John, the mail room's manager, rolled his eyes.

Abby danced into the elevator with a good-natured grin, calling back, "I'm here to save you from yourselves, ladies. He's just not good enough for you." But as the doors closed and she depressed the button for the penthouse, her smile faded.

Admittedly, C. K. Tanner was one of the most gorgeous men she'd ever seen, but he was also one of the most arrogant. He barely acknowledged anyone who didn't have a title attached to their name, and probably hadn't spoken more than two words to Abby in the year and a half she'd been bringing him his mail.

But her opinion of him came from more than just his lack of polite communication. C. K. Tanner was a grown-up version of Greg Houseman, the terribly charming rich kid who'd stolen a poor girl's teenage heart, taken her virginity, then dumped her flat. She knew from painful personal experience that men like C. K. Tanner could be Sir Lancelot one moment and Blackbeard the next. And she would never forget that one rarely came without the other.

She sighed heavily. Lord, she had bigger things to think about than the workaholic Midas who hardly knew life existed below the thirty-first floor. Like how on earth she was going to open her art school on the shoestring her budget would afford her. Granted, her job in the mail room paid her full benefits and allowed her flexible hours—she was out of the office and working on her canvas by two o'clock each afternoon—but the amount of savings she'd amassed wasn't even close to what she needed.

Every day she was receiving more and more calls from parents who desperately wanted their children in an art class but couldn't afford the steep tuition at any of the art schools in town. The community center where Abby taught didn't have programs for kids, and they'd told her emphatically that if she wanted to start one it would have to be held somewhere else. Now she had a waiting list a mile long and only a few thousand dollars saved.

It was beginning to look as though her dream would just have to wait a little longer.

The elevator dinged and she pushed the cart down the hall. No spirit-lifting music played on the executive floor, only the low tones of deals being made came from behind the closed doors and throughout the busy hallways. She paused in front of Mr. Tanner's corner office, plastered on a smile, smoothed her hair back, then cursed her Irish ancestry for giving her the thickest, curliest red hair on earth as she knocked lightly on his door.

"Enter," came that same husky command that she'd heard every morning for the past year and a half.

Briskly and with purpose, Abby opened the door

and moved into the room. "Good morning, Mr. Tanner."

He glanced up and smiled. "Good morning."

She hesitated, her brows knitting together. She couldn't remember him ever looking at her before, let alone *smiling*. Swallowing the lump that had just come into her throat, she placed his mail in the wire mesh In basket on the edge of the desk and tried to ignore the spicy scent of his cologne, which always seemed to throw her for a loop whenever she got too close. "Your mail, sir."

His smile widened and warmed. "Thank you, Abby."

She froze. *Abby?* She had no idea that C. K. Tanner even knew her name. What was going on here? And why was he giving her that smile—that unnerving, sexy and very Lancelot-like smile?

Blackbeard, Abby. Think Blackbeard.

"Well, have a good day, sir," she said, turning quickly to go. But the sleeve of her blouse had other plans, catching itself on the wire basket. Laughing nervously, she tugged on the stubborn fabric, trying to free herself. But it wouldn't budge. She gave it one last swift pull, but only managed to send the basket of mail flying. On a gasp, she lunged to catch it, hearing her shirt tear as she landed gracelessly.

With her heart slamming against her ribs and a shaky smile plastered on her face, she raised the basket up in a sad show of victory, only to catch C. K. Tanner's more customary hawk-like stare. Ah, that was more like it, she thought as she leveled her gaze with his own. Trying to pretend that she was calm and unruffled, she stood and set the basket down firmly.

Right onto the lip of his coffee cup.

Suffocating her gasp behind her hand, she watched the dark stain spread menacingly across his desk.

"Ohmigod," she breathed, hearing him rush up beside her. "I'll clean this up right away."

"It's not a problem." His strong hands were on her shoulders, pulling her close to his side and away from the hot liquid, even as he rang for his secretary with the push of a button. "Helen, send housekeeping with some paper towels."

Forgetting who he was and who she was for a moment, Abby glanced up at him—all six feet, two inches of him. Thick black hair, just a little wavy, licked the edges of his starched white collar. Olive skin, chiseled features, full lips and eyes the color of chocolate.

It was a stubborn, arrogant face, but drop-dead gorgeous nonetheless. With that half smile and bedroom gaze, he was the cover of a men's magazine and the star of every woman's fantasy. And he fitted his gray pinstripe suit like nobody's business, while displaying an imposing confidence that permeated the air around him.

She could see why every woman in this building had a crush on him. And why *her* best course of action was to get as far away from him as possible—as soon as possible.

But she didn't move.

He held her loosely against his side, those bedroom eyes now filled with concern. "Are you all right?"

The warmth of him, his strength against her, sent currents of heat zipping through her blood. "I'm sorry, Mr. Tanner. I must've taken a clumsy pill with my vitamins this morning."

Finally he released her and she felt as though she could breathe again. "Don't worry," he said. "It'll be cleaned up momentarily."

As he walked back behind his desk, a woman from housekeeping entered and silently mopped up the mess. She was gone in seconds, and Abby turned to make her own hasty retreat. She wasn't about to hang around and give him time to fire her.

"Please stay for a moment, Abby." His words stopped her and she looked over her shoulder to see him smiling at her—again—his deep-brown eyes roaming her face. *I'll bet he's one great kisser.*

Before she could scold herself for such an outrageous thought, he asked, "Can I get you a safety pin or…"

Abby put her hand over the tear in her white blouse. "It's nothing. I can take care of it." *And I should go.*

"I insist. If you tell me the name of the boutique where you shop, I'll have a new one here in an hour."

Abby tried not laugh. Mostly because it might come out as a wheeze, but also because he'd said "boutique." She'd gotten that blouse for ten dollars at a discount store. "It's not necessary, I have another shirt in my locker, but thank you." Of course, she didn't have anything in her locker but chewing gum and an extra pair of nylons, but she wasn't going to share that with him. All she wanted to do now was get out of C. K. Tanner's office before he gave her two weeks to clear out that locker and never come back.

"How long have you worked for me, Abby?"

Oh, here it comes. "A little over a year, sir."

As he eased into his brown leather chair, he motioned for her to take the seat opposite. "Why don't you sit down for a moment."

Abby bit her lip. "Uh...yes, sir."

"I'd like to talk to you about something."

She perched at the very edge of the seat and blurted it out. "Am I being fired? I'm very sorry about the coffee. And that small fire in the mail room last week really wasn't my fault."

She thought she saw a hint of laughter behind his eyes, but it passed as he said, "I'm going to Minnesota for the weekend to spend some time with the head of a certain candy corporation. I'm interested in buying his company."

Abby cocked her head to the side. Why in the world was C. K. Tanner sharing this information with her? And, Lord, what was the proper response? She opted for a short congratulatory speech. "How...nice for you, sir. I'm sure it will be a very good invest—"

He stopped her with just a lift of his brow. "The catch is, I'm fairly certain he wants the company to go to a family man. And as I'm not married or even in the market to be, I find myself in a disconcerting position." He leaned back in his chair. "Abby, I need you to pretend that you're my wife."

Abby hesitated, blinking with bewilderment, not at all sure she'd heard him correctly.

"Don't misunderstand me. This is strictly a business trip. I need you to act the part of my wife just for the weekend."

Okay, she *had* heard him correctly, but that knowledge brought little comfort.

He crossed his arms over his rather broad chest. "I'm afraid I'm one of those abrupt, come-to-the-point kind of businessmen."

She nodded and managed to choke out, "To say the least."

"You're not married—"

"No, I'm not, but—"

He nodded. "Good. Then I would be honored if you would accompany me to this function."

Abby just stared at him. "Is this some kind of joke, sir?"

He shook his head slowly. "No."

"*You* want *me* to pretend to be your wife for the weekend?"

"Yes."

"And it's just business?"

"Of course."

"Of course," she repeated, laughter erupting in her throat. She couldn't help it. It was all so ridiculous. She came to her feet and took a deep breath. "I'm sorry, but I have to decline."

He studied her for a moment. "Believe me when I say that you will be well compensated."

She stood there, blank, amazed. "You're asking me to go away with you for the weekend and lie about who I am."

He nodded casually, confidently, as though he'd

asked this of a million different women—a million different times—and every one of them had said yes. Well, she wasn't like other women and she wouldn't help C. K. Tanner with his deceitful little plot in a million years.

"My answer is no." She turned and pushed her cart out the door, calling back in the most professional voice she could under the circumstances, "Good day, Mr. Tanner."

Abby McGrady sure had spunk, Tanner mused a few hours later as he opened his door and ushered the private detective into his office. And he didn't know too many women like that. He was rarely surprised by people—even more rarely rejected by them.

And in less than ten minutes Miss McGrady had accomplished both.

She intrigued him. And there was certainly no denying his attraction to her—in spite of that "I just baked fresh cookies and you need to call me if you're going to be late" home and hearthiness. Spending three days and nights pretending they were man and wife would only be possible if he kept reminding himself how much like oil and water they truly were.

Of course, first he had to get Abby to agree to come with him.

Tanner motioned for the detective to take a seat. He'd given the man just three hours to find out as much as he could about Abby McGrady. Tanner already knew she had the right qualifications—smart, quick and attractive—all musts for a good corporate wife. She needed some help with her wardrobe, but that could be taken care of in an afternoon. But her most valuable asset was the fact that her personal—and inexplicable—dislike of him would keep their arrangement totally professional, and that's what he needed more than anything—no strings.

"Her full name is Abigail Mary McGrady," the detective began, his gaze focused intently on the paper in front of him. "She's an aspiring artist. Graduated Los Angeles School of Fine Art in 1998. Teaches an art class Tuesday and Wednesday evenings at the Yellow Canyon Community Center. Miss McGrady has a small apartment close by in West Hollywood where she grows roses in pots on her deck. She buys mint-chocolate-chip ice cream every Friday night after work and she turns twenty-five October the seventh."

"That's this Sunday."

"Yes, sir."

"Anything else?"

"Actually I did find out something that might be helpful."

As he listened to the detective, Tanner felt the corners of his mouth lift into a smile.

Two

The note that had been taped to the door at the start of class was permanently tattooed in Abby's mind.

To all art students and staff:
Unfortunately, due to an overwhelming demand for computer courses, we are forced to cancel art classes for the semester. Next week will be your final class and prorated refund checks will be mailed to you. We are doing our best to bring back this art course next semester. Please accept our sincerest apologies.

Yellow Canyon Community Center

What else could go wrong today? Abby wondered as she waited for her students to finish a watercolor exercise. First she'd spilled coffee all over her boss's desk, then he'd proceeded to ask her to pretend to be his wife for the weekend. And, worst of all, for just a moment when she'd been hypnotized by his gaze, she'd actually been tempted to say yes. With the way her life had been going lately, a weekend of adventure with her gorgeous boss just didn't sound like a fate worse than death.

But that was her lonely heart talking. When her brain wrapped around the fact that this guy was not only a cocky Casanova, he was also her boss, she'd straightened out.

It would be just business, he'd told her earlier that day. Well, of course it would be just business. The man went out with supermodels and actresses who wore Gucci and smelled like eight-hundred-dollar perfume, not a clumsy mail girl who wore clothes from the secondhand store and considered Ivory soap her signature scent.

But one question still lingered: Why her? With all the women who drooled over him, why had he asked her?

Abby sighed and shook her head. It would remain a mystery. By now Mr. Tanner had probably forgotten her name—forgotten she even existed—and found someone else to play his wife for the weekend.

"Everyone done?" she asked the class when several faces appeared over the tops of their easels.

They all nodded.

She exhaled heavily as she stared at the dejected expressions on their faces. "The center can make more money with computer classes, you guys. And this is a slow time of year for them." She smiled weakly. "But I'll figure something out, I promise. Give me a week."

"I can't afford lessons anywhere else," one student said.

"Shoot, I can hardly afford them here," another added.

Abby nodded. "I understand, but—"

"What if they were free?"

The husky baritone came from the direction of the doorway. The entire room turned to stare, including Abby. Her eyes widened and her heart slammed against her ribs.

C. K. Tanner stood in the doorway, his eyes set on her.

Gone was the pinstripe suit. Jeans and a simple sweater had taken its place. Simple. Hah! Nothing on or about C. K. Tanner was simple, Abby thought wryly, wishing she'd fixed her hair or worn something nicer—something from a boutique.

He moved into the room with the confidence of a general. Tall, dark and sexy as all get-out. And the way he fitted into those jeans had to be illegal, she mused, then quickly told that half of her brain to shush.

"My name is Tanner," he informed the class. "I'm a friend of Abby's."

"Go, Abby," one female student hooted.

Everyone laughed. Abby's cheeks burned.

"He's not a—" she stuttered, then frowned at him, whispering, "I haven't changed my mind, sir."

"Hear me out, Abby," he whispered back. "There's an element to this proposal that might interest you.'' He plunked down beside her on the desk and addressed the class. ''I'm here to offer all of you,'' he glanced over at Abby, ''and you, too, of course, a building where you can hold your art classes. As for the rent—''

''Here it comes,'' muttered one of the students.

''It will be a dollar a month,'' Tanner finished.

Silence. All twenty students stared openmouthed at Tanner, then at Abby, then back again.

Abby's muscles felt like water, but her temper was piqued. The man had some nerve. How dare he come in here and raise her students' hopes like this. How dare he come in here and make their teacher's pulse race. She jumped off the desk and motioned for him to follow. ''Come with me,'' she said, the sound of hoots and catcalls following them as she pulled him out of the room.

Once out in the hallway, Abby whirled on him, ready to give him what for. But her heel caught on the doorsill and she pitched forward into his arms.

Her cheeks flamed. Why did her clumsy nature have to show itself every damn time C. K. Tanner was near? Was she cursed?

''I got you,'' he said in a husky whisper, tightening his hold on her.

Man, he felt good, she mused, steadying herself on her feet. All solid muscle and formidable strength.

Get a hold of yourself, Abby. The guy's a corporate jerk.

''What are you doing here, Mr. Tanner?'' she asked, once she was free from his grasp and a few feet away.

He grinned. "Well it looks as though I'm saving your neck—*and* your class. Now they have a space."

She glared at him. "How did you know we needed a space?"

He shrugged. "Does it really matter? The point is you need one."

Abby couldn't refute that inescapable logic. "I guess I don't need to ask why you're doing this. But right now my students are wondering why. And I'm sure some of them have some pretty...*obscene* guesses."

He raised a lazy brow. "Like what?"

"That's not funny."

"Why do you care so much about what people think, Abby?"

"Why don't you care more?" She looked directly at him, choosing her words carefully. "Look, Mr. Tanner, I don't understand this. Why me? You must have a dozen women who would do this for you."

"I need a stranger," he said simply. "I have no wish for anyone to know about it, nor do I want my...." He hesitated a moment, as if searching for just the right word. "I don't want my female friends thinking the words *C. K. Tanner* and *marriage* belong in the same sentence. Do you understand?"

She nodded. "I'm afraid I do."

"Here. Maybe this will help you decide." He pulled an envelope from his jacket pocket and handed it to her.

With great reluctance she took it and peeked inside with as much unease as if it held a snake.

"It's a contract and keys to a warehouse space

downtown.'' He rubbed his jaw. ''You can pay me the twelve dollars in advance or at the end of the year. I don't care.''

She pulled out the small set of keys, shock slamming through her. A whole building for a year for twelve bucks. What on earth did he expect her to do on this weekend? There had to be more to this than—

As if reading her mind, he answered her silent queries. ''Three days. That's it. I'll probably be down at the plant most of the time. You won't have to see me very much.''

That should have reassured her, so why was every traitorous part of her balking at the notion?

''I'll sleep on the couch,'' he continued. ''In the bathtub—whatever makes you comfortable.''

She rolled her eyes. ''Whatever makes *me* comfortable?''

''Trust me, Abby, you have nothing to worry about.'' His voice was resolute, his eyes sincere.

She buttoned and unbuttoned the collar of her sweater nervously.

He glanced down at the keys in her hand. ''I'm sure you could find many uses for that space.''

Darn right she could. That warehouse would save her art class. And with her own space she could hold classes on weekends for kids, for anyone who wanted to learn. But at what price? She'd be breaking a vow she'd made to herself years ago that she'd never let another Richie Rich invade her life. They were bad news. There was also the added discomfort of having to lie and deceive people she hadn't even met.

But the students, the kids. That was almost worth it.

"You'll sleep in the bathtub?" she asked skeptically.

He held up three fingers. "Scout's honor."

Somehow she doubted he'd ever been a Boy Scout. "Three days?"

He nodded. "Plus time for your makeover and your briefing."

"I have to get a makeover?" she stammered in bewilderment. "What briefing?"

"You need to know all about me, Abby. My habits, likes, dislikes." He hesitated, giving her an appraising look from the tips of her vintage saddle shoes to the top of her unruly mop of hair. "You're a beautiful woman, Abby. God knows why you'd want to hide it. But I think I know someone who can help us with that." He retrieved his cell phone from his jacket pocket. "I'll pick you up at your place tomorrow afternoon at one."

A knot formed in her stomach. "What about work?"

"You have the next two days off." He regarded her with serious eyes. "Courtesy of the boss. Oh, and Abby, I'd like to keep this arrangement confidential."

"Wait just a minute. I haven't said I would—"

He grinned. "Yes, you have. I saw it in your eyes when you held the keys to your new warehouse space."

She ground her teeth, knowing he was right and wishing with all her heart that she could just toss those keys right back at him. But the students, she thought, glancing through the window. They depended on her. And not only that, if she agreed to this farce, her children's program could start immediately.

She looked back at Tanner. His brown eyes practically bored straight through her. Her pulse sped up and she felt sixteen and breathless. The kind of man she'd always vowed to stay away from was going to be her "husband" for three days.

"There will have to be some conditions," she said firmly.

"Of course."

"I'll give you a list tomorrow."

"Can't wait." And there it was. That damn half smile again. "'Night, Abby."

She watched him as he walked down the hallway, cell phone to his ear. Completely unruffled and utterly pleased with himself.

She shook her head, pretty sure she'd just made a deal with the devil. And if he took her soul, she prayed he'd leave her heart intact.

"Are you sick or something?"

Abby rolled her eyes at the suspicious tone in Dixie's voice. It was lunchtime at Tanner Enterprises, and Abby had expected her friend's call, but she hadn't expected the overwhelming desire to tell Dixie about the upcoming weekend with their sexy boss. But unfortunately Abby knew she couldn't say a word.

"Abby, spill it," Dixie demanded. "I can't remember you ever taking a day off since you started here."

Abby sank deeper into her wicker chair as she stared out at the neighborhood's midday activity from the tiny deck attached to her tiny apartment. "I have a really bad headache, that's all," she quickly explained. It was the truth actually. A headache that hadn't gone away since yesterday's mail route had taken an unusual little twist. Well, a major upset actually. And now here she was, waiting for C. K. Tanner to pick her up for a makeover.

She was crazy to agree to this. Truly. No matter how they dolled her up, she wasn't sophisticated or chic. She was the poor relation at best, and she wondered if she'd get through this weekend without serious damage to her self-respect.

If she could just forget this whole thing, she would. But last night she'd told her students that their class would continue. And this morning she'd called every last parent on her waiting list to tell them that their children would have a place to study art. The deed was done.

She was so deep in thought, she barely heard Dixie ask what she was doing for her birthday. "So, Abby, what'll it be? Chippendales or club hopping?"

Birthday. Oh, Lord. Sunday. She'd be in Minnesota. Thank God her parents were out of town and they'd had her birthday celebration last weekend. Having to make excuses to them would be virtually impossible.

"I'll be hiding under a rock," she muttered, her mind searching in vain for another excuse when Dixie came asking again—which, of course, she would.

Dixie snorted. "Why you hate birthdays I'll never know. Perky people are supposed to love birthdays."

"I like other people's birthdays. It's just when I'm the one getting older—"

"You're turning twenty-five, for goodness sake." Dixie sighed. "I don't think that qualifies you for Grandma Moses status yet."

Abby laughed. "It's not a vain, getting-wrinkles sorta thing, Dix. It's a productive thing. I really wanted to have the art center up and going by now. And—"

She halted midstream. Having her very own art center was exactly what was happening. No more excuses or feeling sorry for herself. She was going to have her dream fulfilled—and all because of C. K. Tanner.

"You'll get there, Abby," Dixie was saying. "One day at a time, you know? Hey, I know what would make you feel better."

"I'm almost afraid to ask."

"A date," Dixie exclaimed. "Better yet, a *man*."

"What's the difference?" she couldn't help saying.

"A thousand miles, hon." Dixie chuckled. "A man sticks around—he's a boyfriend, a husband."

Down the street the wind kicked up leaves with a flourish, announcing the arrival of a gleaming black Mercedes that Abby could only assume was C. K. Tanner's. This was a modest neighborhood, where understated Spanish homes sat quietly bracketed by smallish apartment complexes. It was a tan Ford kind of neighborhood, not a luxury full-size.

Abby felt her heartbeat pick up speed as the car

slowed to the curb in front of her apartment. The windows were tinted a light smoke color, but she knew it was him. The driver's side door opened and he stepped out, looking unbelievably handsome. Damn him.

You need a man, a husband, Dixie had said. Abby stifled a laugh. If her friend only knew that she was going to have a husband for three days, and it was none other than the mail room's fantasy, C. K. Tanner.

"Listen, I'd better go," Abby said, coming to her feet and stepping back into her apartment. "I've got to take some, ah…some more aspirin."

"Will you be in tomorrow?"

"Ah…I'll see how I feel."

"Sure you don't want me to bring you anything? I have an hour for lunch."

Abby's stomach dipped as she heard Mr. Tanner's footsteps heading down the hall. "No, thanks. I'm good. Just lots of bed rest."

"All right, hon. How about a birthday lunch with the girls and me on Monday, then? We'll continue the celebrating."

"Perfect."

"And don't think you're getting off the man subject so easily."

A knock at the door caused her to jump. "Sure thing, Dix. I'll call you."

She ran to the door, swinging it wide. "I'm sorry for not meeting you downstairs, sir, but…" Her words trailed off as she took in the man leaning against the doorjamb.

"No apology required," he said, his smooth baritone filling the space between them.

Her stomach dipped. "Would you...ah...like to come in?"

"Sure. For a moment." He inclined his head. "See how my wife lives."

Wife! Abby cleared her throat, and tried to stop her gaze from raking over him as he walked confidently into the apartment. Black jeans encased his strong legs and a ribbed black sweater molded to his torso, accentuating his muscled chest and broad shoulders. Some odd sense of pride welled within her, as though he belonged to her, but she quickly pushed such a ridiculous thought aside. Remember why this man's here—why he's *hired* you, she chided herself.

"Can I get you anything, Mr. Tanner?" she said, trying to sound light and cheerful. "Coffee, soda?"

"No, thanks."

She watched him walk around her apartment, looking at her knickknacks, artwork, furnishings and books, assessing. He stopped in front of one of her paintings. An abstract acrylic portrait of a man with normal features except for his eyes. Where pupils should have been there was only a deep shade of gray.

"This is an exceptional piece," he said. "Who's the artist?"

She grinned in spite of her nerves. "I am."

He hesitated, his gaze remaining on the painting. "You're very talented, Abby."

"You sound surprised, sir."

He shook his head. "Impressed. Maybe even the smallest bit envious. I can recognize extraordinary art when I see it, purchase a gallery filled with it if I wanted to, but—'' he chuckled ''—I can barely draw a stick figure.''

''Well, some people have the art gene and some have the business one, I guess.''

''You certainly have the art one in spades.'' He moved closer to the piece. ''And who's the subject?''

''A man I knew a long time ago.'' Abby went to stand by him. ''He had trouble seeing.''

''He was blind?''

She nodded. ''In a way.''

He turned to look at her then, his brown eyes probing, searching, making her uncomfortable in both mind and in body.

She swallowed and took a step back. ''Shall we go?''

After a moment's hesitation, he nodded, and Abby went to gather her things.

They were out of the apartment, down the stairs and walking toward the car when Tanner moved slightly ahead of her to open the car door.

''Thank you, sir,'' she said, trying not to sigh when she sat down on the plush leather seat. The interior of the car was immaculate: no candy-bar wrappers, no coffee cups. The leather looked polished, brand-new, and nary a dust bunny lingered on the dash, or in any crevice for that matter. Perfectly in order, just like the man.

He slid into the driver's side and shot her a look. ''You can't call me 'sir.''' He turned the key in the ignition and the car sprang to life, purring like a purebred cat. "I think it would be best from this moment forward if you called me Tanner."

"Shouldn't I call you by your first name?"

"No one calls me by my first name."

Abby looked up at him curiously. He had his seat belt on, his gearshift in first and his gaze on her. "For the next several days you aren't my employee, Abby. That's certainly not the impression I want Frank Swanson to have of…" A smile tugged at his lips. "Why don't you just call me Tanner, or if you feel a surge of bravery," the smile widened, "honey or dear."

Heat surged into her cheeks at his suggestions, but she barely felt it through a bristling of indignation. "Excuse me for saying so, but I think it's vastly important to remember that I *am* your employee, sir…ah…Tanner."

"Sir Tanner." He put on a good show of considering that as he let out the clutch. "I like it."

Abby couldn't help but roll her eyes as he pulled away from the curb, chuckling.

They were quiet for several blocks, but when Tanner entered the freeway, he broke the silence with business. "When we arrive at the house, you'll have your makeover. I've allowed two hours for this. Then we'll have a dinner meeting and get to know each other. I've decided that we will be newlyweds, just married and trying to keep it quiet. The press keeps tabs on my marital status, so I'll tell the Swansons we eloped." He barely stopped for breath. "This weekend, I feel the conversations should be primarily on business, but feel free to interject…."

As he continued to explain the details and events of the weekend, Abby began to drift off. She couldn't help it—actually what she couldn't help was staring at how his muscles tightened against the fabric of his jeans when he shifted gears.

She knew she had to get a grip and listen to his recitation on business protocol, but it was like being briefed by the Pentagon, for goodness sakes. She decided to find out some information that would *really* be helpful.

"So, who's Frank Swanson?" she asked.

"Have you heard of Swanson Sweets?"

"Are you kidding?" She laughed. "I have at least one bag of chocolate mints and one box of dark chocolate-covered cherries in my fridge at all times."

She had a nice laugh, Tanner thought as his gaze swept her lightly. It moved from high to husky like an ocean wave, causing his gut to tighten. But it was that kilowatt smile of hers—a smile that came from her eyes as much as it did her lips—that had him straying from his "this is just business" commitment. He'd have to watch that.

When the freeway came to an end, Tanner turned right—toward home—the ocean and beach to his left. Automatically he opened his window and breathed in the salty air.

"You must really love candy, huh?" Abby said.

He shook his head. "Never touch the stuff."

"Then why buy the company?"

He laughed.

She opened her window, as well. "Okay, so maybe

that's a really naive question in your world, but I'd really like to know."

He delivered his pat answer without giving it a thought. "It's a profitable venture."

She hesitated and he wondered if she was going to press him for more, but she didn't. Instead, she looked back and forth from the ocean to the palm-tree-lined streets, then turned to him. "You live in Malibu?"

"You sound surprised."

"I just figured you for a Beverly Hills kinda guy, that's all."

"And what kind of guy is that?"

"One who likes to be close to town, close to the action and all the pretty—" she stopped short, her cheeks growing pinker by the second "—the pretty sights."

He couldn't help but chuckle. "Like the La Brea Tar Pits?" Even Los Angeles natives joked about the city's lack of culture.

She was silent a moment before she said, "Maybe you should tell me a little bit about yourself so I'm not guessing. Tell me about your family."

Tanner's mind filled with sharp images he rarely acknowledged, much less talked about: the death of his mother; his workaholic, womanizing father, who had immediately shipped Tanner off to boarding school; his lonely childhood devoid of contact with his father, devoid of holidays in the family bosom; endless days and nights of learning how to control his emotions and become a ruthless businessman.

He cursed silently and told Abby McGrady all she needed to hear. "I'm thirty-two years old. I was born

June twentieth in Manhattan. I run ten miles every morning, prefer whisky to wine and rarely go to bed before two in the morning.''

"Jeez.'' Abby laughed softly. "Talk about a thirty-second life story.''

That was usually enough to satisfy most women he knew. Tanner pulled into his driveway, clearly marked by the Private Property and No Trespassing signs. Certainly it would be enough to satisfy a woman he was only going to know for the rest of the week. "All right,'' he said, sending her a sidelong glance. "How about this for a revelation—this is my first marriage.''

She smirked at him. "No shock there, sir.''

"Abby," he scolded.

But he got no response. She was staring, transfixed, out the windshield, her eyes wide, her lips parted. Full, pink lips that he wanted to run his thumb over to feel, then his tongue to taste.

But he wouldn't.

He shoved all thoughts of her and him and lips and tasting away and helped her out of the car. "What do you think of the place?''

"It's beautiful,'' she said, and if he wasn't mistaken, she sounded a little sad.

"But?''

She raised a brow at him as they walked up the front steps. "But what?''

"I read people's reactions for a living, Abby.'' He held the front door open for her. "I can tell when someone's not telling me the complete story.''

"It's just…so enormous.'' She glanced around,

taking in the black marble floor, chrome and glass accents and circular staircase. "You live here all by yourself?"

He nodded. Damn right he did. In fact, he'd never even brought a woman here. It was his place of solace, to relax, think.

He had a decidedly bacheloresque penthouse on Wilshire Boulevard that he usually used for entertaining. He could've taken Abby there. But he had neighbors who liked to gossip, and the Malibu house had just seemed more appropriate for her makeover and their dinner meeting.

He followed her with his gaze as she moved over to the fireplace and touched the empty mantle gingerly.

"You must not spend much time here." She glanced over her shoulder at him. "There are no pictures or mementos or...anything." She shook her head. "You should do something about that. It's not fair to the house."

He frowned. Not fair to the house? What the hell did that mean? His house was exactly as it should be: comfortable and functional. Just because he didn't have a bunch of meaningless clutter on his mantel like at her place—art supplies everywhere, a million pictures of her family decorating her desk and tables.

He shook his head at her annoying observations. Never in his life had he met anyone who just said whatever was on her mind or asked whatever question popped into her head like she did. People who didn't think before they acted were headed for disaster, didn't she know that?

Hell, it was good that this woman was only going to be around for a weekend.

He nodded at the stairs. "Why don't you go upstairs now, first door on your right. The team's waiting for you."

Her eyes widened. "The team? What team?"

"Your makeover team," he said, turning to go.

"Wow," he heard her say quietly. "It's going to take a whole team?"

With his back to her, he couldn't help but smile at her guilelessness.

"Hey!" she called to him. "I thought you might want to ask me a few questions about myself."

"Later. At dinner," he replied succinctly as he reached the door. "I have work to do."

It was only partly a lie, he thought as he turned in the doorway and watched her walk up the stairs, her hips swaying gently with the movement. He did have work to do, always had work to do. But this time he was using it as an excuse to get away from the pretty redhead who was threatening to drive him crazy.

Three

"**D**arling, you have wonderful bone structure." The makeup artist, who insisted on being called "La George," clasped his hands together, a genuine look of relief on his face as he studied Abby's features. "Not to mention a gorgeous head of hair."

Wanda, the hairstylist, nodded and smiled. "You really do."

Donald, the last member of the team, held several gowns up under Abby's chin. "Great coloring. I think the green strapless to match her eyes. Let's get to work, people." He smiled at Abby. "You ready, Cindy?"

"It's Abby," she corrected gently.

He laughed. "Not today, darlin'. Today, it's Cindyrella."

Abby couldn't help smiling at them, her team, so

excited about their task. She tucked a wayward and very wet curl behind her ear, then pulled her robe closer around her. They were a nice lot and she wondered if they knew the reason for this makeover. She guessed not. C. K. Tanner wasn't the most open person on earth, she thought, remembering his brief essay on himself in the car earlier.

Short and to the point, his little background report on himself probably left out some pretty interesting details.

But then again, she had some interesting details of her own she wasn't about to share with him. Like how much that sophisticated, charming demeanor he displayed reminded her of the act Greg had used until she'd finally believed that he'd loved her, too, and had given him the most precious gift she could give a man.

She let out a sigh. Why was she even comparing the two people or the two situations? This wasn't high school, and her boss had no interest in her other than business.

La George smiled down at her, his eyes glistening, lip liner poised and ready. Truly, this was no romantic endeavor. But if her makeover team liked thinking of her as Cindyrella, she wouldn't enlighten them further. She'd let them have their fun, and maybe let herself have some, too.

As Wanda plugged in curling irons and blow dryers, Abby gazed about the room. If ever a storybook had come to life, with people, props and costumes, this room would have been beyond the author's imaginings.

It was a den of some sort and quite different than the downstairs. Where that was modern and cold, this room was warm and inviting. Its very presence in the austere house made its owner even more enigmatic than before, and Abby wondered for a moment what else besides a cozy room lay hidden beneath C. K. Tanner's cool, calm, collected and ultraprofessional exterior.

Tall ceilings, dark-blue wall hangings and worn, comfortable tan leather chairs. Bright sunshine blazed a trail to the spectacular ocean view from the windows that made up one long wall. A large, tan sofa with two cushy pillows tucked into its corners faced a brick fireplace several steps above the roomy dressing area, where Abby and the team were assembled.

Her stomach clenched. Again, she wondered if she'd be able to pull this off. Wife to millionaire playboy, C. K. Tanner.

"Chin up," La George commanded, a powder puff in his hand.

Solid advice from the makeup artist. That's exactly what she'd do. Because her future and the future of her art school were riding on it. She'd simply keep her chin up, be herself this weekend, do the best she could not to embarrass herself or Tanner and pray that the candy man believed them.

In the entryway mirror, Tanner straightened his chocolate-brown Armani tie, shrugged into the matching jacket, then glanced at his watch. Good God, two and a half hours. What were they doing up there? He'd knocked on Abby's door more than twenty minutes ago, but Wanda had told him she wasn't ready yet. He shook his head. She was already a beautiful woman—she didn't need that much help, for heaven's sake. He was almost afraid to see what they'd done to her.

Upstairs a door opened, and Tanner heard several voices whisper and giggle. Then the sound of high heels on the wood stairs echoed throughout the foyer.

"Finally," he mumbled under his breath, then called out, "I don't know if you're a wine drinker, Abby, but I opened two—"

His voice broke off midsentence as he stared open-mouthed at the vision that was slowly descending the stairs. Gone were the baggy clothes and the mop-top hair. Her green eyes flashed fire, reflected in the emerald silk dress cut just below the knee and just above the bust, accentuating a soft curve he'd only imagined she possessed. Her hair, which had usually been up or hidden, fell past her bare shoulders in rich, red curls. And then there was something he couldn't have seen—Abby McGrady had legs that went on for days. Heat surged into him, circling, landing deep in his groin.

She reminded him of a damn Botticelli painting. Innocent and sexy at the same time.

She looked like trouble.

He muttered an oath as he realized for the first time what he'd done. He'd picked a woman who didn't want him—a woman who aggravated and intrigued the hell out of him—a woman who was beginning to make him question his own rules about "good girls."

She reached the bottom step, smiling at him a little nervously. "What do you think?"

Images of creamy skin, tangled limbs and red hair blowing in the ocean breeze flashed in his mind. Stay cool, boy, or you're cooked. He closed his eyes for a moment, then opened them, feeling in control once again. "You look fine, Abby."

Abby felt her eyes widen, her cheeks turning instantly scarlet. She looked down at her shoes. *Fine?* She'd just spent hours being plucked and curled and powdered, and the man had the nerve to tell her she looked fine? She didn't expect him to tell her she looked stunning or anything, but *pretty* would've done it, or *really good.*

Abby sighed inwardly. Oh, who was she kidding? She felt gorgeous for the first time in her life and she wanted him to tell her so. She wanted him to tell her that she looked beautiful—as beautiful as the models and actresses he dated. But what she got was "fine."

He's your boss, Abby. You're not here to get compliments, you're here to work.

Tanner raked a hand through his hair, his jaw tight. "We should talk."

"All right," she said with the most professional nod she could manage.

"Dinner's almost ready." He turned and headed down the hall. "Come with me."

Sure, this was a business thing, she reminded herself as she followed him down the hallway, through room after room. This wasn't real. Tanner wasn't her husband, this wasn't her home, and she didn't normally wear two-inch strappy sandals and a killer

dress. But for the next several days she would, she
did. She truly felt like a princess, and she was going
to make the most of it.

"I'd like to show you something," Tanner said
moments later as she followed him into what appeared to be his office. It was a gorgeous room, she
thought, if you like the cool, clean, sparse look. Tall
ceilings, white walls, impersonal artwork and a stone
fireplace that looked as though it had never held a
fire. And once again, there were no special items, no
photographs of anyone anywhere.

With its view of the ocean, open sliding-glass door
and billowing curtains, she was certain she'd seen its
like on the cover of *Architectural Digest.*

And what a view, she mused, stepping outside on
the balcony and breathing in the sea air. The show
that Mother Nature was putting on tonight was spectacular. Sheets of red blazed across the darkening sky
like the fuel tracks of a fighter jet—its mirror image
a cool pink displayed below on the ocean's surface.

"Abby?"

She turned sharply, realized she'd been lost in
thought and left the balcony. "You must love living
by the ocean."

He smiled and said, "I do," then took out a velvet
box from the top drawer and placed it on his desk.
"I have rings for us."

Abby froze. *Rings?* She hadn't even thought
about—

"They belonged to my grandparents," he said,
opening the box.

Abby gasped as she caught sight of a beautiful,

pale-yellow diamond ring and the plain platinum band next to it. "No, I don't think—"

"We're newlyweds." Tanner raised a brow at her. "It would look a little odd if we didn't wear rings, don't you think?"

She drew in a deep breath. Of course he was right. It was something she hadn't even thought about, a minor detail that C. K. Tanner would never miss. But the intimacy of it took her by surprise. His grandmother's ring on her finger. It would make this whole charade feel authentic. Every look he gave her, every glance or smile, it would make her feel connected to him. She didn't want that, but what else could she do?

"Don't you like it?"

She bit her lip. "It's not that," she began, but found she couldn't finish the thought. Like it? Of course she liked it. It was exquisite, a delicate cluster of yellow diamonds set in platinum. She touched it reverently.

"If it's a larger stone you want, I can arrange that." His voice was suddenly so cool it made her shiver.

"No," she insisted, glancing up at him. "It's beautiful and exactly what I would've chosen."

His eyes softened. "I hope it fits." He picked up the ring and held it out to her. "May I?"

Something told her to grab the ring, put it on and scamper out of his study like the frightened little forest creature she was. But she stayed put.

He took her cool hand in his warm one. An ocean breeze rushed into the room, upsetting papers and caressing Abby's neck just as Tanner slipped the ring on her finger.

"It fits pretty close to perfect, I'd say." He brushed his fingers back over her freshly manicured nails, smiling. "This is a nice color."

She swallowed the frog in her throat. "It's called Temptation."

"Well, it certainly is that."

She looked up at him, searching the shadows of his face, her pulse pounding at the base of her neck. What now? What was she supposed to say now as his gaze blazed down into hers, gold fire and pure heat?

He lifted a brow. "My turn."

She just stared at him. "Excuse me?"

"The ring."

"You want me to give it to you?"

He chuckled hoarsely. "You sure have a way with words, Abby."

Heat surged into her cheeks. If she wasn't bumbling with her feet, she was doing it with her mouth. "What I meant to say was—"

"Don't worry, I know what you meant." He slipped the platinum band on his finger unceremoniously.

Abby cleared her throat. "So, how does it fit?"

His eyes twinkled. "A little tight. But I think I can handle it for the weekend."

Somewhere a bell chimed. A soft, tinkling sound that only just nudged her from her dreamlike state. Then it chimed again.

Abby dropped her gaze. "Someone's here, I think."

"No." He smiled knowingly. "Dinner's ready, Mrs. Tanner."

Her stomach flipped over at the intimate words and the husky sound of his voice. Soft, low, caressing. She was falling hard and fast for this whole charade. She needed to remember that Cinderella turned back into a poor servant girl at midnight—or in this case at the end of the weekend—and that the looks Prince Charming tossed her way were only part of his practiced act.

Tanner glanced across the candlelit table and reminded himself once again that he'd chosen Abby McGrady to *work* for him, not to tempt him or captivate him or make him laugh. But tonight everything seemed off kilter.

Seldom had he had a formal dinner without the bustle of waiters and the constant chatter of other patrons to keep him from focusing on his companion. Nor had he had such interesting conversation. Books, music, art, food, wine. But then again, when he asked a woman for a date he wasn't exactly looking for conversation.

He picked up the bottle of merlot and held it out to her. "Another glass?"

She shook her head. "I'd better not. More than one glass and I can get…well, let's just say I want to keep my head about me." She looked up at him. "Have you ever had too much to drink, Tanner?"

He nodded. "Once. In college. Then never again."

"I'm willing to bet that you couldn't stand that relaxed, out-of-control feeling."

He leaned toward her and whispered conspiratorially, "Well, if you call waking up in a fountain on campus relaxed, I'd have to agree with you."

She laughed. "You didn't."

"Oh, yes, I did. Right beneath a large metal statue of our college's founder." He had no idea why he'd just shared something so foolish with her—gotten personal. But he did know that her company was bringing out an entirely new side of him. One he hadn't known was there. And it bothered the hell out of him.

She wiped her mouth daintily, then placed her napkin over her plate. "Since you chose to show me one of your scars, so to speak, it's only fair that I do the same."

At this moment, Tanner thought, he'd love to see anything she wished to show him. Creamy skin, beautiful shoulders, long legs. Wherever she had a scar, he'd love to find it.

Snap out of it, Tanner. You're acting like a damn teenager. This lady's off-limits.

Forcing back the surge of desire that had his body in a chokehold, he continued their playful repartee. "Did you wake up in a fountain, too?"

She laughed and shook her head. "Far more embarrassing."

"Well, spill it."

She drank the rest of her wine, then took a deep breath. "I went to the art academy here in town for four years. My family cut all kinds of corners to help pay my tuition, but there was never enough money left over for books and art supplies."

Tanner leaned back in his chair. "Don't tell me your scar is selling plasma for extra money."

"That's not it." Her cheeks were flushed, and she didn't meet his gaze. "I was an artist's model."

A forest fire erupted inside Tanner. He tried his damnedest to avoid conjuring up the image of her, nude, standing center stage in an artist's studio. But he failed. "You..." he stammered, which he never, ever did. "You modeled nude?"

She lifted her chin defiantly. "It's art, Tanner. It's beautiful."

"I bet it is."

"And, as hard as it is for you to believe, not sexual."

"Uh-huh."

This line of conversation had to end or he was going to spend the rest of the night—and possibly the morning, too—under the spray of an ice-cold shower.

He cleared his throat. "Didn't you say something about a list of conditions last night?"

She nodded slowly. "I didn't actually make a list. I just thought that we could be as respectful of each other as possible this weekend. I know that this situation dictates a certain amount of touching. So, I've decided that a little hand-holding and an occasional kiss is acceptable."

"Agreed," Tanner found himself muttering, his mind running a mile a minute with questions like, Where was he allowed to kiss her on those occasions? "Anything else?"

"Yes, actually." She smiled at him. "I reserve the right to make up other conditions as I go along."

They both stared at each other for a moment, until Abby broke out in laughter, followed by Tanner, and the tension eased greatly, much to his relief.

"You know, I can't wait to see Minnesota again," she said.

"You've been there?"

She nodded. "My aunt used to live on Lake Minnetonka. I love it there. Especially now in the early part of fall. With all the different colors of leaves, it's like a work of art every time you step outside. Don't you think?"

She took a sip of water, and Tanner couldn't help but follow her hand with his gaze, watching his grandmother's ring as it winked in the light on Abby's finger.

"Regretfully, I've only been to the airport."

"Oh, that's too bad. They grow the best apples there. Each bite tart, sweet, then tart again." Abby looked out the picture window at the moonlit ocean, her eyes sparkling. "I wish I could have an apple tree. But you saw the deck on my apartment."

Dammit. Her perfume, that clean, soft scent that clung to her skin, was slowly turning his mind to mush. And that creamy white neck of hers seemed to be calling, begging for a kiss—

Snap out of it, Tanner! he told himself. Abby McGrady's marriage material and your employee. A very dangerous, very undesirable combo.

His housekeeper set their desserts in front of them with a smile, then quickly departed. Crème brûlée. Tanner glanced up to see Abby's reaction to the elegant dessert, but her gaze was downcast.

"Is something wrong?"

"No. Not at all. It's lovely."

"Abby."

Abby fought the urge to insist that the pretty cream-colored concoction in front of her looked appetizing. She didn't want to hurt the housekeeper's feelings or appear unsophisticated. But she had no clue what it was and they'd been honest with each other up until now—maybe even a little too honest—but what the heck.

"Okay, to tell you the truth," her voice fell to a whisper, "I'm not much into fancy-dessert-type things."

He smiled and whispered back, "I think there's some ice cream in the fridge."

"Now you're talking." She stood up and offered him her hand. "I've got a great idea...."

Five minutes later, with his jacket off and his tie loosened, Tanner stood in front of a large bowl of ice cream. Abby had given the housekeeper the rest of the night off and turned the whole kitchen upside down, coming up with lots of goodies. Sliced bananas, chocolate sauce, crumbled cookies, marshmallows and raspberry preserves were laid out in several small bowls.

Tanner looked eager and excited, like a little boy who'd just heard the siren song of the ice-cream truck tooling down the street after school.

"Okay." Abby tucked a napkin into the starched collar of his shirt and one into the top of her dress. "Let's dig in."

"There aren't any nuts," Tanner pointed out.

Abby pointed to a small bowl. "But we have chocolate sprinkles." She gave him a knowing look. "And you have to learn to love chocolate."

"I do?"

"Of course you do. It's your new family business."

"Right." He said the word, but his eyes said something entirely different—something she couldn't make out.

She didn't press him. Instead she poured some of the sprinkles on his ice cream, laughing at his shocked expression.

They quickly prepared and consumed their sundaes. Abby devoured hers swiftly and with gusto, while Tanner ate his slowly, savoring every bite.

When he was finished, Tanner licked his lips. "Best damn dinner meeting I ever had." He smiled at Abby, his eyes dark and promising. "Thanks for the suggestion."

Does he look at a woman like that before he kisses her?

Her knees feeling exasperatingly like Jell-O, Abby turned away from him and started tidying up the kitchen, wondering how in the world she was going to get through a whole weekend of those looks, that voice, those eyes and that smile.

The ocean looked haunting at night, Abby thought, gazing out the open car window as Tanner shifted gears and pulled onto the Pacific Coast Highway. The salty air permeated her nostrils and the breeze calmed her. She had to admit, in this one thing she envied him. She glanced over at him. He was watching the road, his stubborn jaw brushed with stubble, the sexy shadow making his lips look full and darker in color.

She turned and stared straight ahead. Okay, so she was attracted to C. K. Tanner. What did that make her? Just one of the thousands who were ready to throw themselves at his Gucci-shod feet? No way. Not her.

Tonight had been… Lord, what had it been? Not exactly a barrel of monkeys, but fun—and fascinating. She hadn't bumbled or broken a single thing. Instead, she'd had the makeover of a lifetime, gotten a little tipsy, told one of her deepest, darkest secrets and found out that the in-control C. K. Tanner wasn't always so controlled. She hated to admit it, but after tonight, she was looking forward to this weekend just as much as she was dreading it.

"You should've brought the dress home. I wanted you to have it." Tanner palmed the gearshift and swung into Fifth, the muscles in his forearm flexing as he moved.

Soft shivers passed through Abby, and the jeans and blouse she'd changed back into after they'd gobbled up dessert suddenly felt confining. "I don't attend functions like this very often. Well, not at all really. The dress has no place in my closet, but thank you."

He nodded. "Well, I'll have it packed up for you along with all the other things George picked out. I don't know if there will be much cause to wear an evening gown in Minnesota, but who knows. You should always be prepared."

She looked up at him. "Did you learn that in the Boy Scouts?"

He pulled up to the curb in front of her apartment building and set the parking brake. "I was never in the Boy Scouts."

She laughed. "Is that so?"

Damn, he liked hearing her laugh. She wasn't like anyone he'd ever known, and he had that same inexplicable urge to pull her into his arms and kiss her, once, just to see what she tasted like, but he fought against it with everything he had.

He turned off the engine. What the hell was the matter with him? She was cute and funny, but she delivered his mail. They were from completely different worlds. No possible way was he thinking what he thought he was thinking. No way. He was keeping this thing strictly business—even if it killed him.

And if their time spent together was anything like tonight, it just might.

He walked around the car and opened the door for her.

She didn't move. She just blinked up at him.

"What's wrong?"

"I'm stuck." Her voice was only a notch above a whisper.

He leaned against the doorjamb. "Excuse me?"

"I'm stuck. I'm stuck," she repeated somewhat frantically. "My hair's caught in the headrest. Lord, I hate these foreign cars."

He shot her an amused grin. "You get yourself into these situations pretty often."

She glared at him. "Is that a question?"

He crouched down beside her. "A statement." He studied the seat. "How exactly did you manage to do this?"

"Can we maybe discuss my foibles and the history of them at another time? I need freedom. I have a sort of borderline claustrophobia-type thing."

"That's a shocker," he muttered on a chuckle. "Can you arch your back a little?"

Her eyes widened in alarm. "Why?"

"So I can reach up behind you. I don't want to hurt you."

She arched her back as much as she could—which was about three inches away from the seat. Tanner eased his hand behind her, grazing the warm, soft skin of her neck in the process. He closed his eyes for a moment, trying to gain control over his raging libido. But he could still smell that damn perfume of hers. Hell, he was turning into a jackass teenager.

He inched nearer to her—his head resting dangerously close to her breasts as his fingers wound around in her long, soft, curls, searching for what held her.

"Do you feel it?" she asked hoarsely.

He practically groaned, his body on fire. "I think so." Slowly he pressed the headrest up and helped her out of the car.

Abby felt her heart thud against her ribs as they stood on the curb for a moment, the wind kicking up leaves around them just as it had that morning. It was as though nature electrified whenever they where together. Ocean, leaves, wind, all conspiring to create this unrealistic mood.

She touched the band on her finger. "Would you like your ring back or—"

He smiled at her. "No, you hold on to it."

She nodded. "All right."

They walked to the door, an awkward silence filling the air.

"I have to say that I'll be glad when this is over," Abby said, opening the door to her apartment building. "I hate lying."

"It's not my usual style, but it was a necessary evil this time, I'm afraid."

She turned to face him, her back to the small lobby. "Isn't it possible that you could get this company on your own, Tanner? Show Frank Swanson who you really are?"

He stared into her eyes, green pools of appeal, and thought how easily a man could get lost there. "No. I have no desire to show *anyone* who I am."

"But when he finds out that we're not really married—"

"He won't." He raised a brow and smiled at her. "By the time the ink is dry on the contracts that make Swanson Sweets mine, you and I will be divorced."

Abby stiffened. "You say that so easily, like the institution of marriage is meaningless."

"To me, it is," he said curtly. He wasn't going into his opinions about marriage right now or ever. That was his business, and because Abby McGrady had two parents who were still married and obviously loved each other and their children, she would never understand, anyway. "I'll pick you up at seven tomorrow morning. We have an early flight. Good night, Abby.''

He headed toward his car without looking back. Marriage was a charade, just like tonight, tomorrow and the next several days. If he had his way—which he usually did—he'd be single forever. He climbed into his car and gunned the engine. He wasn't going back to the beach tonight, he'd sleep at the penthouse.

That is, if he could sleep at all with the scent of Abby's perfume still lingering about him, on his clothes, in his mind.

Four

"**W**e should be landing in an hour, Mr. Tanner," the flight attendant whispered.

He nodded at the woman. He was afraid to move any more than that lest he disturb Abby, who lay fast asleep in the crook of his arm. She'd been so exhausted when he'd picked her up that morning, he wanted her to rest as much as possible. They had a full weekend ahead, and if they were going to pull off this charade they needed their wits about them.

She hadn't said a word about the way they'd parted last night, and he was grateful. He wasn't interested in rehashing the matter of marriage or continuing the debate on acquiring the company. Damn, when she was around he wasn't exactly sure what he was interested in or what he wanted.

She wasn't what he was used to. She wasn't what

he'd expected. Truth was, something had happened during that dinner last night. He'd had a good time for the first time in a long time...with no pretense. And it sure didn't have anything to do with candles or flowers or ice-cream sundaes.

He glanced down at her.

After takeoff, they'd exchanged a few words and she'd asked if she could take a short nap. She'd been asleep ever since.

When was the last time he'd held a woman like this? Tanner wondered, brushing a wisp of shiny red hair off her cheek. Or better yet, when was the last time he'd wanted to hold a woman...or felt comfortable enough to stay this close to her?

She looked like an angel in her angora sweater and cream pants. A pain-in-the-neck angel, he mused, remembering the emerald glares she'd shot him at the community center the other night. She had fire in her.

Tanner inhaled sharply. Damn, what he wouldn't give to feel that fire beneath him.

The scent of her shampoo wafted up to greet him. *Apples.* The girl sure loved apples. Maybe he'd give her a small tree as a present when this whole thing was over.

Suddenly the plane pitched to the left, tearing him from his thoughts. Instinctively his arms tightened around her.

The captain came on the speakers. "Sorry about this, Mr. Tanner. We're experiencing some unstable air. Should clear up in a few minutes."

And even as the captain spoke, the plane lifted and plummeted violently.

Abby pushed against him and sat bolt upright. "What's happening?"

Her words were slurred slightly, but he could hear the panic in her voice. "Just a little turbulence. Nothing to worry about."

The plane jerked sideways, then again.

"Ohmigod," she said, her voice quavering. "We're going down."

"Look at me, Abby."

"What?"

"Look at me."

She did as he told her and, eyes wide, said, "It's something you couldn't know about me. I'm terribly afraid of flying. Actually, it's more that I'm terribly afraid of crashing."

Her voice was sluggish, her eyes glazed. Tanner looked at her closely. "Did you take something?"

She nodded. "My doctor told me to take it right before we took off."

Once again the plane lifted and fell.

Abby gasped and shut her eyes tight. "We're going down."

Tanner tightened his hold on her. "Everything's okay," he whispered softly, stroking her neck and back. "It'll stop soon. Just keep your eyes on me."

She was shaking, her fingers gripping his arms.

"Abby, nothing's going to happen to you as long as I'm here, all right?"

Slowly she opened her eyes and nodded tentatively. She kept her unfocused gaze locked on him. They remained like that for several seconds, and Tanner felt something pass between them. Something he didn't recognize and probably didn't want to acknowledge. After a moment the plane stilled, but Abby didn't break the connection.

"I'm not sure what to do now," she said.

She looked like a vulnerable kitten, ready to be comforted, ready to be kissed. And he could no more deny her than he could himself. He lowered his mouth to hers and gave her a gentle kiss.

He heard her breath catch, and he fought the urge to groan. She tasted sweet and hot, like honey, the way he'd imagined, and he wanted more. He wondered if she'd pull away, wouldn't blame her if she did. But instead she grabbed his collar and pulled him closer.

Temporary insanity reigned and he answered her call, capturing her mouth again and again in a rhythm of soft kisses. And when she parted her lips for him and he traced their soft fullness with his tongue, an intense agony of longing barreled through him.

"Tanner," she breathed against his mouth.

Something snapped, deep in his gut. Maybe it was the desire in her voice, maybe she just felt too damn good, too damn right. And maybe it was the fact that she had taken something and wasn't thinking clearly.

He muttered an oath, maybe two, and released her. "You need to sleep."

And I need to get the hell away from you before I forget that this is a business trip.

She stared at him for a moment, her eyes turning from glazed passion to confusion. Then she dropped her gaze and nodded. "All right, Tanner." Grabbing her pillow, she turned away from him and settled against the window.

Tanner dragged his gaze away from her and opened his briefcase. Work. That was the best thing—the best distraction a man had. But if he got one ounce of work done, it'd be a miracle. He could still taste her, feel her mouth on his, and he wanted more.

He gripped the sides of his leather case. He wasn't going to have more. Sure, he'd gotten carried away for a minute. But he was no cad.

He mentally reviewed the myriad of reasons why he couldn't turn back to her and pull her into his arms: she was the marrying kind, he'd promised to restrict their contact to little more than hand-holding, and she was hopped up on some kind of sedative just so she could be here with him.

Knowing it was a bad idea, he glanced over at her again. She looked so soft and sweet with her small hand tucked under her cheek, but he'd felt the passion in her, the hunger.

He was acting like a fool. Experienced women with no ambitions for home and hearth were his thing. He didn't have time for helpless, innocent females.

He muttered an oath. With one damn exception, it seemed.

I'm never trusting doctors again, Abby vowed as she stared out the window of the limousine that was whisking them to the Swansons' home. With a little pharmaceutical assistance she'd become a relatively stress-free flyer that morning, so relaxed and uncon-cerned with the possibility of crashing to the ground

in a ball of fire that she'd fallen asleep almost as soon
as the plane had taken off.

Until the gut-shaking turbulence hit, of course.

And until she'd allowed Tanner to kiss her.

Allowed, hell. She'd *wanted* him to kiss her. And,
in fact, right now more than anything she wished he
would lean across the limousine's smooth leather seat,
take her in his arms and kiss her silly and senseless
for hours as the cool Minnesota breeze kicked up
leaves and pelted them against the car.

Abby swallowed hard. She hadn't been so drugged
that she couldn't recall the softness of his lips, the
way he moved his mouth against hers, the way every
inch of her tingled at his nearness and touch. But the
kiss had been a momentary lapse in judgment on both
their parts. For Tanner it clearly was. He'd been the
first to pull away. And right now, after her spectacular
appearance at the Swanson Sweets plant, being close
to her again was probably the farthest thing from his
mind.

*And who could blame him? You just made an ab-
solute fool of yourself.*

Still groggy and a little sedated when they'd arrived
at the candy factory some two hours earlier, Abby
had pulled a "Lucy and Ethel" on the tour that Frank
Swanson had set up for them. Only minutes into the
visit, while walking through the chocolate area, Abby
had tripped on some boxes and pitched forward into
a tub of chocolate cream.

She felt her cheeks burn as she recalled how Tanner
had helped her up, her hands, and the front of her
sweater covered in the sweet-smelling confection.

He'd emerged with one of his Versace suit sleeves coated with cream as they both stared at the impression she'd left in the chocolate. The only thing that salvaged her pride was when Mr. Swanson said sympathetically that things like that can happen from time to time around sweets. "You've heard of the call of the wild?" he'd said with a chuckle. "Well, this is the call of the chocolate."

Short and burly, with a salt-and-pepper beard, infectious smile and eyes like Santa Claus, a kinder, sweeter man than Frank Swanson simply didn't exist. And if she hadn't already promised that warehouse space to her students and the kids, she would've called a cab right then and there and gone straight back to the airport.

"Do you need another towel? You're still looking a little sticky."

Startled, Abby glanced up at Tanner. "No, thank you."

"You're sure?"

He'd removed his chocolate-stained jacket and washed his hands thoroughly. Sitting against the black leather seat, he looked spotless and in control, as always, but his expression was unreadable, and she couldn't tell if he was still angry at her or not. Odds were, he was.

"What I could use is one of those back scratchers for my whole body," she said, trying to muster a smile. "I think I'm allergic to sugar. On the outside, that is."

He gave her a dry smile over the top of his paper. "That's very funny, Abby."

She threw up her hands. "I'm sorry, okay? How many times do I have to say it?"

"I'll let you know."

She shifted in her seat. "This is really all your fault, Tanner."

He raised an amused brow. "And how would that be? I certainly didn't push you into that tub of chocolate cream."

"You forced me to come with you."

"Hardly forced." He shook his head and laughed. "Just try to keep out of trouble and vats of candy for the rest of the weekend."

She rolled her eyes. "I'll try to be more like the perfect corporate wife. A silent, simpering, doting, yes-woman."

Silence filled the affluent air of the limousine, and she wondered if she should apologize again. Oh, who cares? she thought. He doesn't like you, anyway. You've already blown it. That kiss was just a fluke.

Tanner glanced up from his paper, his eyes hooded like a hawk's. "We both know how far from that description you are, Abby. Besides, that's not the kind of wife I'd want, anyway."

Abby felt her brows rise. "What kind of wife do you want, then?"

Tanner hesitated, astonished by the words he'd just said, then dropped his gaze back to his paper. "Having none at all suits me fine," he muttered, hardly seeing the article on the fluctuation of the Euro he'd been trying to read for the past five minutes. *Wife.* What the hell had made him even say something like that—and to her?

He didn't lead women on. They knew what he wanted and didn't want. And after that kiss he and Abby had shared on the plane, the last thing he wanted to do was give her ideas that he was interested in a real marriage.

Damn, she aggravated him something fierce. She could've cost him Swanson Sweets with her antics today. But she hadn't. Instead she'd endeared Frank to her.

Tanner rubbed at the stubble on his chin. What Abby didn't know was that when she'd gone to the ladies' room to wash up, Frank had turned to Tanner and gone on and on about her. How he loved that she wasn't one of those silly women who couldn't get their hands a little dirty, how one of his own kids had taken a tumble into the chocolate—on purpose, of course—but Frank felt that her dip into the chocolate cream was the rite of passage of a true chocolate lover. And before Frank had left ahead of them in his own car, he'd warned Tanner not to let go of such a wonderful woman.

Tanner peered over the top of his paper at Abby. Why hadn't he told her what Frank had said? Why was he acting annoyed? Maybe because he *was* annoyed. Shoot, if he'd pulled something like that, fallen into a vat of candy, if he'd put one toe over the boundaries of propriety that he'd carved out for himself, he'd never be where he was.

But, amazingly, Abby's little antics charmed everyone around her. Her students, the workers at the Swanson Sweets plant, Frank—they liked her, and Tanner envied that. He could intimidate or coerce, but very few people liked him—very few people even knew him.

He couldn't help but smile as he watched her. Even with chocolate smudges marring her skin and clothing, she was beautiful and too damn sexy for her own good. She was looking out the window, enjoying the scenery, avoiding his gaze, no doubt. It was just as well, he mused, remembering their kiss. He was beginning to think that he'd done a stupid thing by choosing her—now that he couldn't stop noticing how her hips moved when she walked, hearing her laugh, remembering the feel of her mouth against his.

Don't let her go, son. Frank's words rang in his ears ominously. Don't let her go? Hell, Tanner cursed silently. He didn't even have her.

An image of Abby's mouth on his sauntered through his mind.

He cleared his throat and tried to ignore the current of desire running up and down and through him. She had a chocolate smudge on her neck. He saw her pulse speed up as if she knew he was watching—and wanted to taste the chocolate on her skin. Could he make two mistakes in one day?

Slowly he put down his paper and leaned toward her.

In that moment the limousine's glass divider slid down, deterring Tanner from what he was about to do.

"We're here, Mr. and Mrs. Tanner," the limo driver said, passing through black iron gates, crawling up a circular drive and slowing in front of a massive Tudor home.

Curiosity filled Abby as she stared out the window. The Swansons' home was spectacular, and she wondered how anyone got used to living in such a house. Probably as easily as getting used to being called Mrs. Tanner, she thought. Which wasn't easy at all; although, the sound of it was nice and made her stomach do flip-flops. But she knew C. K. Tanner's reputation well, and she'd also heard him loud and clear when he'd said that he didn't want a wife.

So what did it matter to her? She wouldn't marry a modern-day rogue like him, anyway. Great subject for a painting, but not for a soul mate.

Abby practically gasped when she stepped out of the limo and into a vision of autumn. Leaves in shades of rusts and yellows blanketed the expansive lawns and silvered concrete. A lovely, brisk wind picked up and she followed its path. Surrounded by trees, a pretty little lake was just visible in the distance. And, in front of her, under a deep-blue sky, stood the house. Ivy crawled up the walls of the gray stone mansion, bracketing the windows like a verdant picture frame.

Suddenly the massive door opened and Frank and a pretty, plump woman—who Abby could only assume was Mrs. Swanson—came down the steps to greet them, holding each other's hands, both smiling from ear to ear. They reminded Abby of her own parents, full of love and adolescent romance. Frank had told her that he and his wife had been married thirty-two years and still held hands under the table at dinner. Tanner had probably never even held someone's hand when crossing the street as a child.

A thread of anxiety ran through her. Could two people who were so much in love spot two others who barely knew each other?

As though he could feel her trepidation, Tanner placed an arm around her waist. Unconsciously she pressed against him, leaning into his strong, solid frame.

The woman reached out and took Abby's hand. "I'm Jan Swanson. Welcome to Minnesota. Can I call you Abby?"

Abby returned the smile. "Of course."

Jan patted her hand. "And you'll call me Jan." She looked up and at Tanner. "You must be Tanner."

He smiled at her. "It's nice to meet you, Jan. Thank you for having us."

"It's our pleasure," she said. "I wish I could've met you earlier, but Frank's filled me in."

Frank winked at Abby. "All good, I promise."

"Then he must've left out my chocolate nose-dive," Abby said without thinking.

Tanner cleared his throat.

"What I mean is…" Abby said, letting her words trail off, her face growing hot in spite of the cool day.

"Oh, sweetie," Jan said on a laugh. She leaned in and whispered, "That's how I knew I'd like you so much."

Abby beamed as Frank slapped Tanner on the back. "Come with me, son. The driver will bring your bags in. I've got something to show you in my work-room." He turned to his wife and Abby. "We'll see you two later."

Abby glanced up at Tanner. He smiled down at her,

his gaze unusually playful. "Will you be all right without me for a while, sweetheart?"

Her breath caught at his look and the endearment, but she managed to utter, "I'll try."

"Men," Jan said when they were alone. "They always think you need them, when it's really the other way round. But of course, we never tell them so. Don't want to burst their masculine bubbles, do we?"

"No, we don't," Abby said as she followed Jan into the house, trying not to think about how Tanner didn't need her. How he didn't need anyone.

"How many times have you seen *Willy Wonka and the Chocolate Factory,* son?"

Tanner stared at Frank as they stood in what could have been an oversize toolshed at one time, but had been revamped to resemble a miniature version of the Swanson Sweets plant. Bright lights, candy-making contraptions, small assembly line.

Willy Wonka? His mind raced back to his childhood. Visions of oompa-loompas and everlasting gobstoppers flitted through. He'd seen that movie in school, but he couldn't recall the exact story. "I saw it as a child. Friday night was movie night at my boarding school."

Frank nodded. "I went to boarding school, too. Back East. It could be pretty lonely at times."

"Well, that's certainly changed," Tanner said lightly. "You have a big family now."

"My wife, my children—they were my saving grace." Frank smiled at him. "You'll find that out."

Tanner nodded slowly. "Yes, sir."

"How many do you want?"

"How many what?"

Frank laughed. "Children."

His chest tightened, and he wondered at the physical reaction to such an easy question. "Abby and I really haven't decided."

"It's a challenge, that's for sure. Probably the biggest one either of you will ever face. But the rewards are something else, Tanner." His eyes softened. "No acquisition or hostile takeover can match it."

Tanner nodded stiffly. Normally CEOs didn't get personal or philosophical. He was damned uncomfortable. In fact, this whole conversation bothered him. He didn't mind being alone and he wasn't looking for a wife or family to save him. His father had been married and had a child, and he hadn't been able to get rid of Tanner fast enough.

"You're an intelligent businessman, Tanner." Frank leaned against a metal cabinet. "You've probably gathered by now that this weekend wasn't just for recreation. Yes, I want to get to know you and Abby better, and I want you to know us."

Tanner nodded. "We've been looking forward to it. Hopefully, we'll find some time to talk a little business. I brought a full plan—" Swanson's expression was enough to stop him midsentence.

"Besides getting acquainted, there's something else I want from you, Tanner," Frank explained. "It's a tad unconventional. I don't know if you're up to the task."

A muscle worked in Tanner's jaw. "Name it."

''In the three days you're here, you'll have free rein of this workshop.''

''For what purpose?''

''I want you to design your own piece of candy. A Tanner original.''

Tanner felt his brow furrow. ''I'm not a chef. You can't expect me—''

''I expect you to try,'' Frank interrupted. ''It doesn't have to be perfect, Tanner. I'm far more interested in creativity.''

''Look, Frank. I'm a businessman.''

''I understand that. But the other buyers who want this company have a creative streak, a sense of play.'' He regarded Tanner with a serious gaze. ''I want to see yours.''

Tanner didn't know whether to laugh or curse. The man was serious. Creativity? Hell, ask him the long-term sales projections for each of his many companies and he'd have numbers in ten seconds. But invent a piece of candy? Frank might as well have asked him to carry the New York Stock Exchange on his back.

''You can present the candy at Sunday dinner, when all the other potential buyers are here.'' Frank turned off the workroom lights and headed toward the door. ''Abby can assist you, but no other outside help. I must have your word.''

Frustration coiled through Tanner. Obviously, if he wanted the company, this was part of the deal. He reacted the only way he knew how when a challenge was shot his way. He nodded his agreement.

Had a bath ever felt so good? Abby wondered, sinking farther under the bubbles and deeper into the tub. It wasn't short and shallow like the bathtub in her apartment. No, this sucker had claw feet, was deep as a Jacuzzi and had a soft, cotton bath pillow to rest her head on.

It was funny. She'd never imagined that she and Tanner wouldn't be staying inside the Swansons' house. A room in the inviting mansion would've been wonderful, and far safer for two people who were playing married and had just shared their first kiss on a plane. But Jan had insisted that the ''newlyweds'' have some privacy and had ushered Abby down to the small, beautiful guest house across the lake. Complete with fireplace, comfy couches, handmade rugs and a king-size bed, the cabin was far from rustic.

It reeked of romance.

Abby sank even lower until her chin rested on the steamy surface of the water. Her cheeks and her stomach had warmed at the sight of that bed. What was happening to her? She couldn't be interested in someone like Tanner. Sure, he was great-looking and sexy—and what a kisser—but she knew firsthand that the sons of wealthy families only played with girls like her for a night of fun.

Sure, C. K. Tanner was hard to resist, but she'd just have to stand firm.

Taking a deep, calming breath, she relaxed back against the pillow and closed her eyes. Dinner wasn't for a few hours yet and Tanner was busy doing his businessman thing. She had time to relax.

Tanner could almost feel the smoke coming out of his ears as he stalked down the stone path toward the cabin Frank had pointed out. Candy making? The man was nuts. Perhaps that's what was driving him to retirement. Insanity.

When he reached the front door of the guest house, he didn't knock. He strode into the room and glanced around, looking for Abby. Frank really seemed to like her—perhaps she could talk with him, get him to change his mind about this ridiculous test of fitness to own Swanson Sweets.

Soft music came from the bathroom, and he headed toward the door. But he stopped short when he heard the sound of splashing water. She was in the bathtub.

"Ah, hell," he muttered as he turned and leaned back against the door. Again water splashed, causing his blood to heat to a dangerous level. He could just imagine her. Eyes closed, lips parted, her red curls piled high on her head and creamy-white skin peeking out from water that was quickly losing its bubbles. In his mind's eye he could definitely make out a shapely thigh and the curve of a breast.

His mouth went dry as sandpaper, but he managed to ground out, "Abby, I need to talk to you."

Abby's heart leaped into her throat at the gruff command. She sat straight up in the tub and looked around.

Tanner.

He was outside the door.

"Okay," she called, stepping out of the tub and grabbing her robe. "Just a sec."

Quickly she checked her face, scrubbed clean, and her hair, wild on top of her head. She shrugged at herself. She wasn't trying to attract him, for heaven's sake. She rolled her eyes at the lie and emerged from the bathroom, pulling her thick cotton robe tight.

Tanner was sitting on the couch, his eyes locked on her, the massive bed the only thing separating them. Suddenly his gaze dropped to the pale-green bedspread, then back up to her.

"Is it time for dinner?"

His eyes darkened.

"I lost track of time," Abby said as she started to ramble. "You sounded a little ornery and I just wondered if maybe you were hungry."

His eyes turned hot, and Abby wondered if any woman could survive for long under that gaze. Whatever the answer, she wasn't moving from this spot. Though the bed was a token barrier between her and the man who made her breathless—it was a solid one.

"Dinner's in a half hour." A slow smile spread across his features. "But it's dessert I need to talk to you about."

Abby felt her eyes widen at his suggestive tone.

"Not to worry, Abby," he said, laughing. "It's strictly business. Why don't you have a seat and I'll tell you all about our new wrinkle."

Five

Whoever said that ignorance was bliss didn't know what the hell they were talking about, Tanner mused ten minutes later as he stared at the closet door—the only thing that separated him from Abby. She was changing out of her robe and into dinner clothes, and he was waiting…and wondering what she looked like every moment. The door was just slightly ajar so they could talk. But he wasn't in the mood to talk anymore.

"I don't see how this is part of our deal, Tanner," she called through the closet door. "Frank wants *you* to create a new candy, right?"

"He's graciously allowed you to help."

"That doesn't mean that I should."

"What the hell are you saying?" he practically growled, his previous thoughts cast aside.

"If you're going to own this company you should know something about the product, don't you think?" She paused. Only the seductive sound of silk rustling came through the door. "Part of the creative process and all that."

"You're talking like an art teacher," he told her with practiced restraint. "Swanson Sweets will be a part of Tanner Enterprises. I'll watch over it, but there will be someone with candy-making experience at the helm."

"I don't think Frank's going to like that."

Tanner snorted and moved away from the door. He didn't need to tell Abby that what Frank liked or didn't like was not his concern. The man was going to retire in supreme comfort, his entire family taken care of for the rest of their lives with the deal Tanner was going to make him.

Afterward, maybe he'd sell to Harrison, maybe not. But, regardless, he'd done this kind of deal a hundred times. He'd always had to prove himself in some way—nothing as ridiculous as making candy—but it was all the same thing, really.

Business. And as long as he did what was required, he didn't care if he pleased some sweet, fatherly man who called him son.

Tanner rubbed his jaw. What had his own father said the one time he'd brought thirteen-year-old Tanner to his offices?

In war, the strong overcome the weak. In business, the strong never allows the weak to know he's being overcome.

It had been the one bit of advice the man had offered that Tanner had adhered to. And, like his father, it had made him a very rich man. Tanner glanced up at the closet door, wondering for a moment what else it had made him. Why didn't his father's pearls of wisdom sound as reasonable as they always had?

He muttered an oath. Abby was trying to make him go soft, and he wasn't going to let her do it.

"Look, Abby," he began. "I may need your help in the kitchen—or laboratory as the case may be— but I'm the boss in the boardroom."

Abby gasped. "That is the most sexist thing I've ever heard. And I'm sure you've said some pretty sexist things in your time."

Tanner couldn't help but smile at that, his aggravated facade lifting. "You couldn't be more wrong."

He hadn't meant his statement in a sexist way, only as situational. He championed women's rights in the office and out. And in fact when one of his VPs had made a slanderous comment about women in business, Tanner had fired him the very next day.

On the other hand, hearing Abby piqued and full of vinegar pleased him for some reason. He cleared his throat and continued in an autocratic tone. "Why do women take forever to get ready? We're going to be late."

"You can go on without me," she said sweetly.

He shook his head. She didn't just sound piqued, she sounded thoroughly insulted. "Look, Abby, I was just saying that I don't need business advice."

"I think maybe you do," she said, a strain in her voice. "We're lying to a wonderful man and his fam-

ily so that you can take a company and— Oh, no.
Ah, shoot.''

"Ah, shoot what?'' Tanner asked quickly. "There
isn't a tub of chocolate cream in that closet, is there?''

"Worse.'' She moaned. "My zipper's stuck.''

"Well, come out of there and I'll help you.''

"I don't think so,'' she said as though he'd just
asked her to walk through a fire.

"Why not?''

"I'm exposed.''

Maybe he *was* asking her to walk through a fire.

"We're two adults, Abby.''

There was a lingering silence from the closet, then,
"You won't look…too closely?''

Tanner stifled a chuckle. "I'll do my best.''

The closet door opened at a snail's pace.

"You may have forgotten, but I *am* your husband,'' he joked, but the laughter died on his lips
when he saw her.

Her hair was pulled back in a loose bun, tendrils
kissing her jaw and neck, framing her face. And what
a face—light makeup, smoky eyes, glossy lips. What
was she trying to do to him? he wondered as his gaze
roamed over her, his chest as tight as the rest of him.

Her knit dress was the color of charcoal and
hugged her gorgeous figure, accentuating her small
waist and the curves of her breasts—just enough to
make a man wonder how soft, how full. Cut just below the knee, the dress showed off her tantalizing
calves and perfectly painted toenails. Why had he
asked the design team to pack clothes like this? Attractive and sophisticated—hell, they were in Min-

nesota. She could have worn boots, pants and flannel shirts and been right at home.

She could definitely drive a man into an early grave.

But what a way to go.

He raked a hand through his hair. "Turn around and let me take a look. It's probably just caught."

She gave him a speculative look. "Something tells me you've done this before. You sound like a professional."

He lifted a brow. "Let's just say it's an acquired skill."

Abby turned, giving him her back, but not before tossing out, "You say that like it's something to be proud of."

"Hold still." Irritation and pure rip-roaring lust circulated in the air around Tanner. Of course her damn zipper couldn't have gotten stuck halfway up her back. Something close to pain passed through him at the sight of her beautiful back exposed from waist to neck, only separated by a thin strip of black lace with one very small hook. And that perfume again.

"Looks pretty bad, huh?" she murmured.

"Killer." Tanner exhaled slowly and reached for the zipper, his knuckles grazing her skin in the process. He heard her sharp intake of breath. Fire ripped into his groin and he felt himself grow hard. What the hell is wrong with me? he wondered. The frustrated query went unanswered as another question came hot on its heels: Was she this soft everywhere?

They damn well better have something stronger than chocolate milk to drink at dinner.

After a few torturous moments, the fabric came loose and he zipped her up as quick as lightning. And just in time. One more second in her company and he'd forget who she was and what she was doing here, take her in his arms and trail kisses down her neck until her pulse raced.

"I'm going to take a look at the lake," he said hoarsely, heading for the door before Abby got a run in her stocking and asked him to fix it for her. "Come out when you're ready."

A look at the lake wasn't going to cool the raging heat that was speeding through him at Mach ten, he mused. A plunge into the lake would be better. And living with Abby like this for an entire weekend, hell, he might have to take a dip every hour on the hour.

The roast lamb, braised spinach and new potatoes tasted like heaven on earth. The wine was light and delicious. And the atmosphere at the oblong dining table was all about fun. A bowl of apples served as the centerpiece and several vanilla-scented candles— perched on side tables and any other available surface—illuminated the dining room.

A smile tugging at her lips, Abby stared across the table at her host and hostess, who sat closely together, side by side. "We've sat this way ever since our first date," they'd explained, promptly placing Abby and Tanner side by side, as well, elbows touching.

Abby tried not to notice how handsome Tanner looked in his fitted blue dress shirt and black suit or how his spicy cologne continually drifted over to her, threatening to suffocate her good sense. And she tried not to remember the exquisite feeling of his hands on her bare skin when he'd zipped her up earlier.

"You're a wonderful cook, Jan," Tanner said as

the older woman poured him a cup of coffee. "Lamb happens to be my favorite."

Jan beamed. "I'm so glad."

Frank poured a healthy amount of cream in his coffee, then looked up and smiled at them. "I wish the kids could've been here to meet you. Kat, our oldest, just had twins eight months ago. I'm afraid between her five-year-old, Cassie, and the new bundles, she and Jon are very busy."

"Maybe another time," Tanner said.

"Oh, yes. I'd really love to see the babies," Abby added gaily, swinging her foot under the table and bumping Tanner's leg in the process.

He put a hand on her knee. Abby gasped, then coughed to cover her surprise.

"Speaking of babies," Frank said, chin in hand, "Tanner and I were just talking about when you two might start a family."

"We...I, well..." Abby mumbled, the whole of her concentration focused on why Tanner's hand remained on her knee and if he knew how her body was reacting to just that simple touch.

"We need more married time," Tanner offered, glancing over at her.

A lock of jet-black hair had fallen over one eye, and light stubble darkened his jaw. He really was sigh-worthy. She smiled weakly at him.

"Frank, leave them alone," Jan scolded, patting her husband's hand. "They just got married, for heaven's sake."

"Yes, dear." Frank kissed his wife's cheek, then turned and gave Abby and Tanner a big smile. "It'll happen when it happens, I know. Practicing's the fun part though, eh?"

Abby's cheeks burned.

Tanner chuckled and his hand remained on her knee.

Not only were her cheeks burning, but so was the rest of her.

"Frank," Jan scolded. "You're embarrassing them."

"Young people don't get embarrassed." He winked at Abby. "And don't worry about meeting the twins. They'll be at the dance tomorrow night with our kids."

Tanner looked at Abby just as she turned to him. "The dance?" they said in unison, then turned to stare at Frank and Jan.

Frank covered his wife's hand with his own and smiled at them. "We didn't tell you?"

"You're the fox-trot type, aren't you?" Abby called over her shoulder.

"Try salsa and merengue," he shot back. "You better watch out tomorrow night. My dips are reputed to be faint-inducing."

She laughed, breathing in the scents of sugar and chocolate that permeated the air around them. "I'll remember to bring my smelling salts."

The starless night seeped through the windows of the Swansons' laboratory, battling with the warm electric lights for dominion over the room. But tonight, Abby thought, the warmth had won out in both the atmosphere and the man involved in this crazy charade. Gone was the cool front of C. K. Tanner the businessman, and in its place was this incredibly charming man who was starting to get under her skin.

Two hours earlier they'd left the Swansons' house,

changed into jeans and T-shirts and immersed themselves in candy-making activities. Up until now, they'd barely uttered a word to each other, acting as though they were involved in some sort of silent competition.

Back to back, they worked at their stoves, burners and mixtures, trial and many errors causing each to curse under their breath from time to time.

But hey, it wasn't all work. Every time she'd looked over her shoulder to...well, to spy on his progress, she would get the greatest shot of his backside in his faded jeans.

"I'm done. I've completed my masterpiece," she said, seizing the opportunity to take another gander at his beautiful, tight posterior. But the goings-on over at Tanner's stove caught her eye first.

"Holy forest fires." She reached past him and turned down his flaming burner. "You're going to torch the place, Chef Tanner."

"Mind your own business, woman," Tanner said, giving her a wolfish grin as he turned the burner back up. "It needs to be at a high heat."

"How do you know?"

"It's simple physics."

"So was the hydrogen bomb," she said, coming to stand beside him.

"What's your point?" He continued to stir his weird-looking concoction, which looked thick enough to mortar bricks.

Abby couldn't help herself. She burst out laughing.

He switched off the burner, then turned to look at her, his five o'clock shadow dusted with sugar. "It doesn't look much like fudge, does it?"

"It depends," she said with a puckish shrug. "Is fudge supposed to be gray?"

He groaned and handed her his spatula. "Why didn't you try and stop me from using so much powdered sugar?"

"How could I? Think back, Tanner." She drew an imaginary line between them. "'Abby, this is my cooking space and this is your cooking space.' Sound familiar?"

"Vaguely." He glanced over at her pan. "What did you make?"

"It's called a marshmallow mash," she said proudly. "Peanuts, marshmallow, caramel and chocolate. Looks pretty good, if I do say so myself."

Tanner broke off a piece and popped it into his mouth. A crunch and a crackle echoed through the minilaboratory. "I think I broke a tooth. But I'm not sure if it's from the consistency or the sugar content." He eyed the empty bag of sugar next to her stove. "That was full before we started, right?"

Abby punched him in the arm playfully. "Not funny."

He caught her hand, his eyes searching hers. "Who was it again who decided it would be better to make separate candies?"

"You," she said, struggling not to get lost in the brown irises that threatened to hypnotize her. "Trying to show off and impress the ladies or something."

He touched her cheek with the back of his hand. "Just one lady."

They stood only inches from each other, but to Abby it felt like miles, and she wanted him to pull her close.

And while he didn't pull her close, he didn't take his hand away from her face, either.

"From now on, we're a team," he said huskily. "What do you say?"

What do I say?

Frank and Jan weren't here to act as chaperones, no limo driver was going to roll down the partition and interrupt them, no flight attendant was going to check to see if they had enough peanuts. They were alone.

What do I say? I say this is dangerous.

But what came out of her mouth before she could stop it was, "It's a deal."

"A deal, huh?" He smiled down at her, his eyes warm, his hand leaving her face and snaking around her waist. "A deal's not official unless it's sealed with a kiss."

All at once he gathered her up in his arms and covered her mouth hungrily. Abby melted into him, her mind spinning, her breasts tingling as she pressed against the solid muscle of his chest.

She tried to think, to reason. But nothing seemed to matter. She needed this, she needed him.

Her arms went around his neck, and her lips parted, allowing his velvet warmth to invade her as she pressed impossibly closer, feeling the rock-hard evidence of his desire against her abdomen. His urgent, highly seductive kiss made her knees liquid, but that didn't slow her need. She met him every step of the way, their tongues battling for control, their breathing labored.

No man had ever made her insides burn this way, made her feel such longing. In his arms she felt safe. His mouth on hers felt right.

They kissed for seconds, minutes, maybe hours, like two crazy teenagers saying good-night on the front porch for the millionth time. Until Tanner broke away. But only for a moment. To look at her, to catch his breath perhaps. Then his hands raked up her back and into her hair as his mouth seared slow kisses down her neck. She didn't want to be without him for a moment. She pulled his face up to hers again and brushed her lips against his, coaxing at first then demanding, until he captured her mouth once again.

She felt a desire so strong she thought she'd never get enough of him, never get close enough to him. She didn't care what he thought of her or what she thought of herself. In that moment she had the soul of an artist. Restless, reckless and burning. And she wanted him to know that part of her.

"Abby," Tanner whispered almost painfully, easing away from her, his eyes black and heavy with desire. "You make me crazy."

She kissed his cheek softly, then whispered, "Is that really how deals are sealed at the office with your clients?"

His gaze searched hers. "I don't have clients like you."

Abby smiled at that.

Tanner felt his gaze slide to her lips, moist and tinted a rich pink from his kisses. If he didn't back off right now, he might forget all about Frank Swanson's candy-making stipulation. For tonight, anyway.

Romance had never interfered with business before, but right now it was. And what concerned him most was that at this moment he didn't give a damn— about making candy or even about owning Swanson Sweets. All he wanted was Abby in his bed, beneath him, saying his name in that way that made his pulse pound and his restraint disappear.

The thought of tasting her again, tasting every sweet inch of her, almost put him over the edge. But years of steadfast self-control favored the side of business. He needed every minute he could get to focus on work—in this case, making candy—because he couldn't lose this deal.

He forced control back into his mind and body and released her. "We should get back to work. We only have tonight and tomorrow night left."

She nodded, but disappointment shone brightly in her smoky-green eyes. "I'll go get more butter and eggs."

Tanner watched her walk back into the storeroom where the fridge was. His words couldn't be truer. They only had two nights. His fists tightened around the edges of the stove. For candy making, he reminded himself sternly. Not for lovemaking.

Six

Rain began to fall from the night sky. First in droplets, then maturing into thin sheets. The air held a decided chill, but Tanner didn't mind. Stretching out his legs, he leaned back in the wicker chair, breathing in the clean, earthy scent. The screened-in porch of the guest house was the perfect place to watch the rain fall from the gunmetal-gray sky onto the grass and black earth below. It was also the perfect place to return a phone call.

Jeff had called while Tanner and Abby were walking back from the laboratory, commiserating, laughing about their botched attempt at candy making. The call had brought both of them back to reality—why they were here and why they weren't. Tanner's business persona had quickly resurfaced as soon as Jeff had told him he had important news. But talking business in mixed company wasn't Tanner's style, and he'd told Jeff he'd call him back.

Tanner had quickened his pace to catch up with Abby, who'd sped ahead when the phone had rung loudly in the still night air. But it didn't matter who'd been on the phone, the call had spoiled the mood. And when they'd reached the guest house, she'd said good-night to him in a hurry, avoiding his gaze as she slipped inside.

Now, sitting under the protective enclosure, Tanner was dry and comfortable, but not at peace. But whether it was his growing attraction to his sleeping "wife" inside or the phone call he was returning out here, he wasn't sure.

He gripped the cell phone. "It's almost one o'clock here, Jeff. This couldn't wait until morning?"

"I didn't think so. Henry Ward is going to up his offer for Swanson Sweets."

Tanner rubbed his jaw. So, he thought, one of competitors was going to play hardball. "And?"

"To five million."

"Then we'll just offer five and a quarter," he said simply.

"The company's not worth five million dollars," Jeff said brusquely. "Are you sure?"

"I'm not sure about a damn thing today."

Jeff chuckled. "Not going well up there in farm country? Or did I catch you at a bad time?"

A bad time? Tanner didn't think he could ever have a bad time with Abby. Crazy, fun, silly...sexy as hell. Tanner shook his head. He didn't even want to entertain those kinds of thoughts right now. "Everything's fine. Just write up the deal."

"You sound pretty irritable, pal."

"That's probably because you're calling me in the middle of the night."

Jeff ignored that. "So, how's the sparrow?"

"Abby's not a damn sparrow!" The words were out of Tanner's mouth before he could stop them.

"Right, I forgot. You were going to turn her into a swan." Jeff chuckled. "I have to say, this is all very interesting."

"What is?"

"You. Sounds like you're falling for her."

"That's ridiculous." Tanner ground his teeth. "I have to go. Keep me posted."

"Sure."

"Oh, and Jeff?"

"Yeah, I know. I'm fired," Jeff said dryly. "Hey, wait, boss. About Harrison. His people have been on my case all day. He wants Swanson's company pretty bad. And he wants a commitment from us to sell."

The guest-house lights switched off. Tanner felt an almost desperate sense of longing. She was in bed. He wanted to be with her. *You're falling for her.* Jeff's words darted across his mind.

Tanner dragged his hand through his hair. "I don't have anything to sell him yet, Jeff. Just do your usual song and dance until I'm done here."

"Right. 'Night, boss."

Tanner stabbed the End button on his cell phone with force, giving a momentary thought to tossing it into the lake. Why was he so ticked off about Jeff's asinine insinuations regarding Abby? Hell, the guy was just joking around. He'd done that a million times about a million other women.

Why was this one any different?

Thunder answered him. Too late to be contemplating a woman's effect on you, it grumbled. Get inside, go to bed and think about it tomorrow.

"Or don't think about it at all," Tanner muttered, coming to his feet. He grabbed the doorknob and turned it. She was in there, warm and soft under the covers, probably wearing some nightie designed to make a man sweat.

This isn't a romantic vacation, he admonished himself. You're not falling for Abby. You may be so attracted to her your teeth ache, but that's a whole world away from falling.

Tanner turned and looked at the lake once more. Lightning flashed in the sky, illuminating the water's surface like one enormous firecracker.

An explosive night, he thought, opening the front door as quietly as he could. That delicious scent of her assaulted him the second he walked in. All night long, he'd have to deal with her erotic fragrance—and her sleeping so close. What the hell had ever made him think this could work?

Lightning flashed through the window. He glanced around and noticed that she'd vetoed his bathtub suggestion and made up his bed on the couch near the fireplace, only feet away from her. It was fairly dark inside the one-room cottage, but he could just make out her form on the bed. Was she asleep? Could she hear him as he took off his shirt, his jeans? Could she hear how much he wanted to crawl in next to her?

Clad only in a pair of boxers, Tanner lay down on the shortest couch in history, pulled the blanket over him and closed his eyes, all the while wondering...

Is it too cold to sleep on the porch?

Abby opened her eyes and stared at Tanner. Even in the semidarkness she could see how the blanket she'd left barely covered him, how his feet hung over the edge of the couch, how his well-built frame didn't fit too well, either.

It had to be around five in the morning, close to sunup, but dawn wasn't even thinking of breaking. She'd been awake all night, thinking about him, hearing him breathe, hearing him groan as he tossed and turned. He was a big man and he sounded very uncomfortable.

Never having shared a room with a man, she felt edgy. And just the thought of being that close to him made her stomach clench and her heart race. She'd thought about asking him to come up and share the bed with her, but she didn't have the guts. Would he think she was making an overture?

Would that be so bad? she wondered, hugging her pillow tighter. If it turned out anything like the last overture it would be pretty bad. She wasn't a virgin, but she wasn't an experienced woman, either. She'd only been with one man, one time.

The night of high-school graduation. Greg had been drinking, but that hadn't mattered to Abby. He'd told her exactly what she'd wanted to hear, then made love to her. But her penance had come the very next day. He'd not only dumped her, but bragged to all of his friends about how easy she was. Trusting him had been the worst mistake of her life. One she refused to repeat.

She heard Tanner turn over, then curse softly.

Her heart thrummed painfully as she decided what to do. She was no longer an insecure child, desperate for acceptance and love. She was an adult, with a relatively strong will.

She rolled her eyes in the darkness as she remembered how her body reacted to him every time he looked at her. Maybe if they just stayed on their own sides of the bed?

"Tanner?" she whispered. "Are you awake?"

"Yes."

"Are you all right down there?"

"With another five feet of couch I'd be perfect," he grumbled.

"I've been thinking." She rolled onto her other side as outside, lightning crackled, then crashed. "There's a lot of room up here."

"And?"

Abby bit her lip. Just leave it alone, don't ask him. Tomorrow you can take the couch, and he can have the bed.

"Abby?" The frustration in his voice changed to something surprisingly gentle. "You're not afraid of the storm, are you?"

"No, of course not." I'm afraid of being alone with you in this room—in this bed. I'm afraid of never feeling again like I felt when you kissed me.

''That doesn't sound too convincing,'' he said, obviously misinterpreting her tremulous reply. She heard sheets rustling, footsteps, then beside her the mattress dipped with his weight. He touched her shoulder and gently turned her over to face him. ''Does the lightning bother you?''

Abby wanted to look away, but she couldn't. Lightning flashed once again, illuminating him from behind, making him look daunting and dangerous. From deep inside her, a different kind of storm brewed, one she was afraid would never let up. She'd never seen him with so little on, and the sight sent shivers of anticipation up and down her spine. He was glorious. His chest was broad, powerful and she wanted to touch him, pull him down next to her and hold on to him forever.

''I'm here if you need anything, okay?'' He smiled at her. ''Right over there on that two-by-four covered in felt.''

She smiled back at him, her skin growing tight and hot. I need something. I need something, she wanted to shout at him. But then the memory of Greg passed through her mind, and all the feelings of inadequacy, embarrassment and pain poured into her heart. Would Tanner end up hurting her, too? If they made love, would he disappear? Go find a woman in his own world, his own social circle, someone worthy?

Did she really care?

''Abby,'' he began. ''Do you want me to—''

''Yes,'' she finished for him, not exactly knowing what she was agreeing to.

''On top or inside?''

Her breath caught. "Excuse me?"

"Where do you want me to sleep? On top of the covers or—"

"Oh, underneath is fine." She turned over, her pulse racing like a jackrabbit's. "Good night, Tanner."

"Good night, Abby."

She held her breath as she heard him push back the covers. Would their feet touch? Their legs? Their...

Again the mattress dipped with his weight.

Again lightning crashed outside.

Tanner knew he must be crazy or close to it. He wasn't the type to get in bed with a woman who was wearing a little slip of a nightgown to just...*sleep*.

His voice might have been calm when he spoke to Abby, but his body was tight and hard and desperate for her. And she wanted him, too, he knew it. They were both adults. What the hell was stopping him? *Home and hearth, buddy.*

"Better than the couch?" The heel of her foot brushed against him, then jerked away quickly.

"Oh, much," he said, trying to keep the sarcasm out of his voice and the raw desire out of his mind.

"If I kick you or anything, I apologize in advance. My sister and I used to share a bed when we were little. She said I kicked something awful."

"Thanks for the warning."

"But I don't think I'll move much tonight."

"Don't you mean this morning?"

"Right." She was quiet for a moment, and he wondered if she was drifting off to sleep. "Hey, Tanner?"

"Yes?"

"Do you have any brothers or sisters?"

"Nope."

"Where're your mom and dad?"

"My mom died when I was a kid."

"I'm sorry," she said softly.

His jaw tightened. He hated talking about his family—or lack thereof. It was only the present and future that interested him. Not the past, not something he couldn't control.

"Where's your dad?" she asked just as softly.

"He's in France."

She gasped lightly. "Hey, we could call him up and get a recipe. France has the best chocolate."

He frowned. "That's not possible."

"Why not?"

"He's unreachable," he ground out, lifting up his head and punching his pillow. "He's been unreachable for about thirty years now."

She hesitated for a moment. "What if you had an emergency? Do you have any other family?"

"No. And if there's an emergency, I'll go to the hospital."

"What?" She sounded shocked and he could just see her getting her tonsils out with all four grandparents, mom and dad, uncles and aunts, cousins—maybe even the family dog—hovering around.

"Alone in the hospital," she said in sincere disbelief.

He chuckled softly. "I'm a grown man, Abby."

Only the rain beating against the guest house could be heard until Abby whispered, "I'd be there, if you wanted me to."

Shock barreled through him. "Why?"

She sniffed. "We're friends, right?"

Of all the things for a woman to say to him. Why hadn't he picked...dammit, anybody else for this deal? Most of the women Tanner had dated over the years were content to take what they could get. Hell, they weren't around long enough to ask him personal questions. And if by chance a "What's your family like?" was slipped in, they'd stopped immediately when they'd seen the look on his face. But not Abby. She just wasn't afraid to probe further, then offer her friendship.

"Go to sleep," he commanded, dragging his pillow closer, wishing it was her, knowing damn well that they had already moved beyond friendship and into something unknown, uncomfortable and certainly unwelcome.

The storm passed.

And Tanner was up with the sun. Actually he hadn't slept a wink since crawling into bed alongside Abby last night. But that was totally understandable considering that after she'd fallen asleep, her breathing had grown soft and she'd turned over and slipped her arm around him, then buried her face against his chest. It was just too much for any man to bear.

He glanced down at her, extraordinarily beautiful in the morning light. Her hair feathered across the pillow and her cheeks were stained with pink. She wore a thin, cotton nightgown with little purple flowers all over it. And one ruffled spaghetti strap had fallen off her shoulder, revealing the curve of her breast to his gaze.

Tanner swallowed hard. Thank God he hadn't been able to see her clearly in the darkness when he'd gotten into bed last night. Even with the dreary talk of family, he didn't think he could've controlled himself.

In the long hours between darkness and dawn he'd figured out what was stopping him from making love to her. It wasn't just because she trusted him or that she considered him a friend or that she was marriage material. No, that obviously wasn't enough for a man like him. It was an altogether different issue.

Truth was, he wanted her like he'd never wanted any woman before, and that was a problem he didn't want to face. Abby McGrady truly wanted something more than breakfast in the morning. Maybe a wedding ring, an "I love you" or, at the very least, the promise of a relationship. Tanner gritted his teeth. He couldn't give that to her.

Incredible. He'd run straight into the fire of a million-dollar deal, but one pretty and very quirky girl made him feel uptight and damned confused. What he needed was some serious exercise.

Careful not to wake sleeping beauty, he slipped out of bed, put on his sweats, grabbed his shoes and headed out the door. A run always eased his mind and whatever else was ailing him. Or it had in the past, anyway.

"What are you going to wear tonight?" Jan asked Abby as she steered the grocery cart down the bakery aisle in search of blueberry bagels.

"I haven't decided yet," Abby said with a smile, though she didn't feel much like it. Tanner had been gone when she'd woken up that morning and when he'd returned, sweaty and worn-out, he'd barely said hello before telling her that he'd be down at the plant with Frank all day. Then he'd disappeared into the bathroom, and soon after, she'd heard the shower water blasting as noisily as last night's rain.

Last night.

Abby bit her lip. Something had happened last night besides the intensifying of an obvious attraction. First she'd seen his playful side when they'd attempted candy making, then his profound, wounded side when they'd talked about his father. It looked like Tanner wasn't really the cold, hard shell of a man she'd thought him to be—or the distant, unemotional businessman he wanted everyone to think he was. Little by little, without even meaning to, he was sharing himself with her, and she was drinking it in.

But obviously, the sharing was over. It was quite clear to her that he didn't want the friendship she'd offered in the wee hours—or anything else she had to offer for that matter.

After his brush-off, she hadn't waited for him to get out of the shower. She'd gone up to the house and found Jan halfway to her car. With nothing to do but think about Tanner until the dance tonight, Abby had accepted Jan's invitation to go grocery shopping. And, she thought, watching the older woman scan the bakery aisle for the perfect morning bread, it had been a wise decision. Jan was a hoot.

Jan picked up a bag of bagels and tossed it into the

cart. "If you don't have any country-western-type clothes, I could get one of my girls to lend you something."

"Country-western?" Abby said, her brows drawing together.

"It's a square dance, honey."

The image of Tanner in cowboy gear put an instant and very genuine smile on Abby's face. Her guess was that he didn't know a thing about square dancing, and all his boasting about salsa and merengue wasn't going to do diddley out there with "Swing your partner and do-si-do."

Abby followed Jan into the frozen-food section. "I think I have something suitable to wear. There are no cowboy hats in my suitcase, though."

"I'll get Frank to loan Tanner one," she said, scooping up a bag of frozen peas and heading down the aisle. "There's nothing sexier than a man in a cowboy hat."

"I don't think Tanner could get any sexier," Abby said without thinking, momentarily overcome with nostalgia as she spotted her beloved frozen pink lemonade.

Jan turned the corner and headed into canned goods, calling back, "So, are you a friend of Tanner's or do you work for his company?" Then she squealed with delight. "Corn Niblets!"

Abby felt her stomach fall into her shoes. She ran ahead, trying to catch up with Jan, knocking down several cans of stewed tomatoes in her haste. "What did you say?"

"Corn Niblets. Frank loves them."

"No, the other part."

She paused and turned, looking Abby straight in the eye. "You mean the part about you and Tanner not being married?"

Abby felt her eyes widen, then she groaned. "How did you know?"

Jan laughed. "Oh, honey. I have two kids. You learn to spot fudging a mile away."

Abby swallowed hard. "Does Frank know?"

"I don't think so. If he does he hasn't told me." She turned and pushed the cart down the aisle. "He doesn't notice the details."

"I'm so sorry," Abby began, following her. "If it wasn't for the…I wouldn't have agreed to…we'll be gone as soon as I tell Tanner—"

Jan whirled around. "Don't you tell him a thing." She grinned. "This is the most fun I've had in a long time. Besides, we have to give him time enough to realize he's falling in love with you."

Abby just stared. "What?"

Jan grabbed a bag of chocolate chips from a nearby shelf and opened them. "So, when did you realize *you* were head-over-heels?" She thrust the bag of chocolate toward Abby.

Abby waved away the chocolate chips and stared at Jan. "I'm not head-over-heels. I don't even…"

Jan popped some chips in her mouth and raised her brow.

Abby sighed and looked away. "All right. Yesterday, maybe. No, last night when we were making candy."

Jan's smug smile made her look like the cat that

ate the canary. "Ah, yes the candy making. That was a damn good idea of mine."

"That was you?" Abby laughed, then quickly sobered. "It doesn't matter what I feel for him, Jan. It wouldn't work. We're the fish and the bird."

Jan's brows drew together in a puzzled frown. "What are you talking about?"

"You know that old saying. Fish, bird, where do they build a nest? Or how?"

Jan munched on her chocolate, shaking her head. "That's a bunch of hogwash, honey. That bunk is for people too darn scared of being hurt to take a risk."

Jan sounded just like Abby's own mother, and she couldn't help but smile as she shook her head. "He doesn't even like me."

"You're wrong about that. Take it from a woman with eagle eyes and a mystic heart." She put her arm around Abby's shoulders. "You and me, we come from the same stock. Family, love, commitment...it comes as natural as butter to us. But to a man like C. K. Tanner, it's Greek." The confusion must have shown on Abby's face, because Jan lowered her voice to a conspiratorial tone and said, "You see, I've done a little digging. Tanner's practically an orphan. His mother died when he was little. His grandmother raised him until he was seven, then she died. His father couldn't give a damn for anything besides chasing an endless stream of pretty young things around Europe. Tanner's been in boarding schools, on his own, relying on no one for most of his life." She eyed Abby seriously. "You can't expect him to recognize what's best for him at first sight."

A deep ache curled around Abby's heart. She wasn't surprised to hear these things about his past, his hurts. But the wish to ease them was strong.

This time when Jan offered her some chocolate chips, Abby took a handful. "You have this all worked out, don't you?"

"I believe in giving people a chance to prove themselves. Show what they're really made of." Jan winked. "And that doesn't just mean C. K. Tanner. This challenge includes myself, my husband and you."

Seven

Evening had come again and the beginnings of fall made the air crisp. But inside the Swansons' massive barn, Tanner noticed, the mood was all about warmth and hospitality as the Autumn Dance got under way. Bales of hay were stacked in uneven heights, jutting out from the walls, serving as both extra seating and decoration. Funny-looking scarecrows sat amongst the guests at long tables covered with checkered tablecloths, while little pumpkin lanterns hung from the ceiling. *Homey* and *festive* best described the scene. But *cool* and *distant* were the words that best described his ''wife.''

Abby wasn't exactly ignoring him, he thought irritably. But neither was she being particularly attentive. His gaze followed her as she and one of Frank's daughters, Kat, made their way toward a refreshment table, laden with everything from homemade lasagna to lemon bars. Not that he could blame her after the way he'd acted this morning.

On his run, he'd made up his mind to be detached and removed with Abby. It was his only chance to curb his attraction to her, he'd thought as his feet had pounded the mossy ground around the lake. But his resolve did little to block how pretty she'd looked when he'd returned from his run, her eyes bright and her hair falling in waves about her shoulders. Fresh and clean and wearing her robe, she'd looked good enough to eat. But he hadn't missed how her eyes had lost that brightness when he'd walked past her to the bathroom, saying short, brisk words that resembled the way he spoke to an employee he hardly knew.

And it seemed to be divine retribution for his behavior that he hadn't been able to think about anything else *but* her all damned day. At the Swanson Sweets plant, he'd acted more like a mopey teenager than the head of a corporation. While Frank was explaining conveyer length or the restructuring of the operators that worked them, all Tanner could hear was Abby whispering those words that still surprised him.

"I'd be there, if you wanted me to," she'd said, her back to him as they snuggled under the covers.

Tanner's attention came slowly back to the present as he followed Abby with appreciative eyes as she joined a group of Kat's friends. Damn, she looked great in red. Her candy-apple T-shirt was snug in all the right places, he mused, his gaze raking the length of her. And were jeans supposed to fit a woman so well? he wondered as he noticed how the denim encased her long legs while embracing her smooth hips. And where the hell had she found those boots?

"Wow!" was the only word that came to his mind, and from the looks on the male faces of the group, he wasn't the only one who thought so.

Something close to annoyance passed through him at that thought. But what claim did he have over her? She wasn't his wife, she wasn't even his girlfriend. He exhaled heavily. What was wrong with him? He wasn't a jealous kind of guy. And, he reminded himself for the hundredth time, Abby McGrady sure as hell wasn't his type.

He shook his head in surrender. All right. He wanted her. In a way Jeff had been right. Not about the falling for her—love was just not an option or even a possibility in his life. But when she was ignoring him this way, he was miserable. And when he was away from her, he didn't feel right. To put it simply, he missed her. Her company, the way she talked about everything all at once, her laugh. Even at ten yards away, across a crowded dance floor, he missed her.

"You look mighty dashing in your duds, cowboy."

Tanner glanced over his shoulder and spied Jan coming toward him. He touched the tip of his borrowed Stetson and gave her a smile. "Thank you, ma'am."

She came to stand beside him, her gaze following his. "Sweet girl you got there. Smart, too."

"She sure is."

"I'd say you picked yourself the perfect wife."

She had no idea. "I'm a lucky man."

Jan regarded him intently. "She's just as lucky."

Tanner chuckled. "Well, much obliged, ma'am."

Jan cocked her head to side. "My curiosity is getting the better of me. Have you two figured out the Tanner signature sweet yet?

"We're working on it."

She smiled knowingly. "Trial and error, huh?"

"So far it's just error, but we'll get it right eventually."

"I have no doubt of that, Tanner," she said, her eyes sparkling. "I have no doubt."

He smiled, wondering for a moment if they were still talking about candy making, and offered her his hand. "How 'bout a dance?"

"You know how to two-step?"

"I'm full of surprises," he said, drawing her into his arms and giving her a little dip.

Jan laughed. "I certainly hope so."

Across the room Abby feigned interest in one of Kat's friends, a cute, young doctor of something-or-other, named Mark, as out of the corner of her eye she watched Tanner dance with Jan. And she was pretty sure she wasn't the only one looking. She'd seen the way practically every woman in the room had checked him out when they'd arrived. He didn't seem to be aware of it. No doubt he was used to it. And he certainly deserved their silent praise.

She'd expected him to look good in his Western gear, but not drop-dead, mouth-hitting-the-floor kind of gorgeous all the way from the tips of his boots to the top of the worn Stetson that Frank had loaned him.

Thank goodness they only had two more days left here.

But strangely, that thought didn't make her feel any better. She sighed as the music ended and the large group of dancers exited the floor. She still had to contend with the two nights that accompanied those two days.

Mark turned to her and smiled. "What do you say we give it a go? I promise not to step on your toes."

Should I say I'm married? Abby wondered, looking around the room trying to find the man she really wanted to dance with, the man she was hopelessly falling for.

But her spirits sank when she spotted Tanner, a woman on either side of him. They were laughing at something he'd said, and one of them actually had the gall to lean forward and brush her...endowments against Tanner's arm. Couldn't she see his wedding band? Abby wondered, her hands balling into fists at her side. Of all the—

Abby gritted her teeth and eyed the doctor. "I'd love to dance, Mark."

As he guided her onto the floor, the ten-piece band announced that they were going to start the next set with two slow waltzes.

"So what kind of doctor are you?" she asked, moving with him to the music, her mind elsewhere.

"A vet, actually."

"Oh," she said on a laugh. "I thought you worked on people."

"I feel like I do at times." He smiled. "They're like little people. My wife always says that. She's a vet, too."

Abby smiled at that. "Is she here tonight?"

"She should be here any minute. She had an emergency with a little person named Rover. Pretty original, huh?"

Abby laughed again and let the music envelop her. Mark was a decent dancer, and she truly wanted to have fun and enjoy herself tonight. They danced around the room, kicking up sawdust and pieces of hay, and she began to relax. Maybe when she got back to Los Angeles, she'd join a ballroom dancing club, she mused, just as Mark led her to turn under his arm.

But who would be her partner? she wondered suddenly, her heart growing heavy as the waltz ended with a flourish.

Mark spun her out. "Shall we go again?"

"I don't think so, pal."

Abby turned to find Tanner, standing in the center of the floor staring at them, his eyes fierce.

"And you are?" Mark asked with a friendly smile.

"Her husband," Tanner practically growled. "Got a problem with that?"

Mark shook his head. "Not at all." He smiled hesitantly at Abby. "Thanks for the dance."

"That was incredibly rude," she whispered after Mark had quickly departed. "What's wrong with you?"

Tanner slid a hand around her waist and began to move to the music. "Nothing."

"'Got a problem with that?'" she repeated quietly, raising a brow at him. "Who says that? Charles Bronson?" She didn't understand what was wrong with him. Was he jealous? Or was he angry that she wasn't playing the part of his wife properly?

His jaw tightened. "I just don't like seeing you get pawed, all right?"

"We were just dancing, Tanner. Anyway, he's married. And if anyone was getting pawed around here, it was you."

Infuriatingly, Tanner said nothing. Instead he pulled her closer and began to move about the dance floor. The band was playing *Fascination*, a song she dearly loved, and she felt her anger dissipate slightly. So he'd been a little jealous. So had she. She decided to focus on the feeling of being in his arms, moving together to the music.

He danced like a renaissance man. Strong and in-control, a great leader. No shock there, she mused, allowing his movement, his gentle turns, to ease her mind and her aggravation.

They passed the band, which was sitting on the decorated stage amongst pumpkins and baskets of apples. They passed Kat and her husband, picking goodies from the refreshment table. They passed Frank and Jan, who had their grandbabies in their laps. And then they passed Mark, who gave them a pleasant smile and a quick wave.

"Did you even tell him that you had a husband?" Tanner muttered, stopping at the edge of the dance floor.

Abby raised a brow. "Who?"

"Your last dance partner."

"Are we still on this subject?"

His eyes darkened, a muscle worked in his jaw. "If I'd known that you were going to use this trip as an opportunity to go husband hunting, I wouldn't have brought you."

Abby froze, feeling tears spring to her eyes as his cruel words hit her in the gut. No one had ever spoken to her like that. It wasn't jealousy he'd been feeling, she knew now. It was just that he thought his employee was embarrassing him in front of a room full of people.

She didn't want to be here anymore—around Tanner, in this room, on this mess of a trip. She turned away from him, saying nothing, and walked calmly out the door.

Tanner watched her go, his mind applauding his boldness, even while his heart filled with regret. He'd never spoken to a woman with such disrespect. But when he'd seen her dancing with that guy, something inside him had snapped.

What the hell was he thinking? She didn't belong to him. When they got back to L.A. they would go their separate ways, and that meant that she'd be dating, dining and dancing with other men. A muscle flicked angrily in his jaw at that thought. But his anger disintegrated when the image of her face, her eyes glistening with tears, shot through his mind. Tears that he had caused.

That look on her face. He'd never forget it.

Dammit. Why did he care if he'd insulted her? She

was his employee, and he'd best start remembering that.

Turning on his heel, he headed for the refreshment table. What he needed was a stiff drink. What he needed was to forget about business, forget about Abby.

Frank and Jan stood behind the table, munching on brownies. This was not what he needed. No doubt they'd been an audience to the "newlyweds'" fight and he would have to explain.

"Having a good time?" Frank asked him.

"Fine." Tanner stared at the red liquid in the punch bowl. "Got anything stronger than this?"

"I'm afraid not," Jan said.

Frank handed him a glass of punch. "Having a rough night, son? We saw Abby leave."

"I'm sorry about that."

Frank hesitated, his eyes searching Tanner's. "I don't think we're the ones you should be apologizing to."

Tanner bristled. "Look, Frank, Jan—"

"Tanner," Jan interrupted, putting a hand on his arm. "I meant what I said earlier. You're both so lucky to have each other. Don't blow it for something that doesn't amount to a can of soup when all's said and done."

"What are you talking about?"

"Pride."

"Pride's served me well over the years," Tanner threw out without thinking.

"In business, I'm sure," Jan said gently. "But it's just not practical in love."

In love. If they only knew that love, this marriage, all of it was a damned farce.

Frank chuckled. "Hell, son. You acted like a jackass. We all do from time to time. But it's what you do about it that counts." He shrugged and snaked an arm around his wife's waist. "Apart and angry or together and kissing. You make the call."

Damn men. Damn C. K. Tanner for making her heart hurt. Seated on the grassy lakeshore, in the moon's dim light, Abby went over the reasons she'd taken this job. The art school. Of course, the art school. And her students, the kids and classes for anyone who wanted to learn regardless of what they could afford to pay. It sounded so right. It sounded good. But somewhere along the line those reasons for being here had blurred.

It had expanded to include being with Tanner.

But he wanted nothing to do with her. They were both fools, she realized, hearing footsteps approach from the direction of the barn. She wiped her eyes, not wanting Frank and Jan's guests to see her crying. She glanced over her shoulder, and her breath caught in her throat.

He'd come to find her. Her traitorous heart soared for the barest moment before she realized that he'd probably come out here to reprimand her, his employee. He was mad that she'd caused a scene, spurred on gossip, threatened his chance to buy a company he cared little about.

"I've been looking everywhere for you," he said, coming toward her.

She turned back toward the lake, tossing a rock out onto its glassy surface. "Well, you found me."

"Abby, listen—"

She came to her feet, a chilly breeze sending her hair across her neck. "I'm sure I embarrassed you and messed up your chance—"

"No." He exhaled heavily. "I'm an idiot."

She looked up at him then, her eyes wide. "Yes."

"And a fool."

"Yes."

"I didn't mean what I said."

She just stared at him. "Tanner, what do you want from me?"

His eyes searched her face. "What do you mean?"

She shrugged. "I can't seem to do anything right around you."

The corners of his mouth twitched. "You do everything right around me. That's part of the problem."

Her brows knit together.

He waved the silent query away. "You're beautiful and talented and smart and kind and a wonderful dancer." He glanced over his shoulder and sighed. "Back there had nothing to do with you. That was my problem."

She searched his eyes, wanting to believe him, wanting to forgive him. But she feared doing both.

He took a step closer to her, his eyes imploring her to forgive him. "I'm sorry. I swear it will never happen again."

The sincerity in his tone surprised her.

He moved within inches of her and touched her face. "Say you forgive me or—"

"Or what?"

He smiled. "Or I'll have to drown myself in a vat of chocolate cream."

She wanted to smile, to laugh at his attempt to appease her, but she couldn't stop herself from saying the words. "I didn't like seeing you with those women, Tanner."

He paused, then shook his head. "I didn't like seeing you in the arms of another man."

Her heart skipped a beat. "I thought we were only playing roles here."

He looked at her for a long, long moment before he whispered, "So did I, Abby." Slowly his mouth descended on hers, capturing her heat with one gentle kiss. Shudders passed from him to her as she parted her lips. "So did I," he repeated, his lips finding hers once again.

Tentatively, her hands touched his chest, moving upward, around his neck. Tanner groaned and deepened his kiss, taking her tongue into his mouth, sparring, stroking. Even in the cool night air, combustive heat flared, so fierce it surprised her. Her breasts were pressed tightly against the solid wall of his chest, and she could feel the rapid beating of his heart. Or was it her own? She couldn't tell, but she needed him closer, she needed him to touch her.

Abby felt her knees turn to water as his mouth moved to her neck, his burning kisses searing downward, his teeth grazing her throat where her pulse beat violently. She felt out of this world, out of her mind.

Longing for him didn't begin to cover it. Her desire was frantic, uncontained and raw, and she wanted his mouth everywhere at once.

"Tanner," she whispered, her head back, in complete submission to whatever he wanted to take.

He covered her mouth again, his hands raking her back, her shoulders, her neck. Again and again he kissed her feverishly, his tongue playing with hers. Her pulse pounded in her ears as she gave herself over to him, as the cool night air around them intermingled with scents of earth, water and desire.

Weak and confused, she moved with him as he backed up against the base of a tree for leverage. His hands glided up under her T-shirt, finding her tight hot skin that begged to be cooled. She arched against him, silently urging him to touch her, feeling his rock-hard shaft pressing against her abdomen.

His lips found their way to her ear. "Oh, Abby," he murmured, cupping one breast in his hand, feeling its weight as her nipple beaded instantly. Pulling the cotton fabric of her bra aside, he flicked the aching bud between his thumb and forefinger.

Gasping, trying to find her breath, Abby melted against him. A blinding, white-hot pleasure ripped through her, so intense she felt her legs buckle. But she wouldn't give in to weakness. She pressed herself against him, against his erection.

He groaned, his hands searching, one finding her bottom, one flicking open the button of her jeans and dipping inside, finding her wet heat, stroking the swollen ache of her femininity. Suddenly Abby cried out as he slid a finger inside her. Tidal waves of pleasure coursed through her, surging in her blood, everywhere at once, and she moved with him.

"This isn't make-believe, Abby." His voice was ragged, his words explosive. "This is real."

Off in the distance, laughter erupted.

"Someone's coming," she hissed, alarm barreling through her, jarring her from pure sensation. He was right. This was real, but was it right? She had to think, had to have a moment to breathe.

She pushed away from him and ran. Along the water's edge, toward the guest house. She heard him calling her name, his footsteps close behind. But she kept going, even though her heart was back against that tree with him. It was just her mind, her good sense, that—

Suddenly her foot hit a rock. The ground went out from under her. She gasped and pitched sideways toward the lake.

"Abby," Tanner shouted from behind her as she landed on her hands and knees in the shallow water.

Cold water soaked through the knees of her jeans. Mud oozed against her palms, her fingers digging in to hold her steady.

"I'm such a klutz," she whispered to herself, her hair blowing about her face in the breeze.

Tanner was at her side in seconds, his arm around her. "Are you all right?"

"Yes. Just fishing for a husband. You can't leave me alone for a minute."

She made the mistake of looking up into his eyes. They were dark, but humor lingered there.

He smiled, then began to laugh and she joined him.

"I *know,* I deserved that." He took off his flannel shirt, lowered to his knee and draped it over her shoulders. "I'm sorry if I took things too far, back there."

Abby sat back in the wet mud, not caring about the cold water saturating her jeans and shoes. Her skin was still tight and hot and aching from their encounter. Fate was telling her something. Tripping on the rock was like a message from the universe. That she couldn't keep running away from life, from love, from this man. It was a strong message and one she couldn't ignore.

Did it matter that they only had a few short nights together? Did it matter what their differences were? Why couldn't she just let go of the past, enjoy the time they had with no worries, no regrets? Maybe Tanner didn't love her the way she loved him, but he certainly wanted her.

She was a grown woman now, able to make her own decisions. She wasn't going to be afraid to risk her heart anymore. And she wanted this man. Desperately. She had her eyes open to what could be, and she would deal with the consequences later. Tomorrow, whenever they came.

"You're going to catch your death sitting in that water," he said calmly. "And if you'll excuse me for saying so, you need to get out of those clothes."

Abby looked up at him, sitting on his heels beside her, his eyes almost black in the moonlight, his mouth curved into an irresistible smile.

It took her only an instant to decide what to do. "Come here, cowboy," she said, casting aside his

Stetson and grabbing him by the back of the neck. Yanking on his clothes, she pulled him down next to her with a splash, feeling his weight pitch forward into the inky water.

"You deserved that, too," she whispered, her lips meeting his hungrily. "And this."

"I readily take all punishment, Mrs. Tanner," he said huskily, returning her kiss, hard and restless. After a moment he broke away, rising onto one soggy elbow. "I want you so damn bad, Abby." His jaw was tight, his voice suddenly unsteady. "But you need to tell me you're sure. Knowing everything you do about me, I need to know you're sure."

She gave him a slow smile. "I've never been so sure about anything in my life."

Quick as lightning he was on his feet. He gathered her in his arms and moved toward the guest house with the speed of a panther stalking its prey. Only a few yards, and he was at the porch, covering her mouth with his as he opened the door.

"Are you cold?" he asked, shouldering his way inside and setting her on her feet.

She couldn't take her eyes off him. "A little."

"I'll take care of that," he said, easing off her T-shirt as she unbuttoned his jeans, each stealing little kisses as they worked to free each other of the constraints of their clothing.

Wet clothes flew in opposite directions until they were both naked, their hands grasping at each other, frantic, desperate. He paused momentarily, looking at her, his eyes wild and hot. No man had ever looked at her with such sweet intimacy, and she felt no embarrassment. Instead his gaze made her feel charged and cherished.

"You are so beautiful." His voice was husky as he gathered her up in his arms, his hands caressing every inch of her as his mouth found the sensitive spot behind her ear. Abby couldn't get enough of his warm skin or of the way he was touching her. Her hands went around his waist and grabbed hold of his backside, pulling him toward her.

Tanner groaned. "You keep doing that and I'm going to lose control."

"Promise?" she whispered, baiting him with her hips, arching against him.

He chuckled softly and eased her back onto the bed. The cool sheets felt like heaven against her hot skin, and she was reminded of the night before, and how differently this one was going to play out. She was lost in him.

When had that happened? What did it matter?

All questions, all thoughts disappeared, were lost as he moved over her, his mouth finding her breast. She cried out as he took the tight peak between his teeth, then rolled his wet tongue across it in seductive ritual. She felt powerless but strong, and she wanted more. He smelled tangy, like earth and lake water, and she felt drawn to him like moon and tide. She plunged her hands through his hair as he moved his delicious torture to her other breast, laving, suckling her nipple, his hands grazing up her thighs to her waist.

"You make me crazy," he whispered, his breath tickling her breast, destroying her restraint.

She arched her hips up, her nails digging into his skin, into his muscles. "Please. I need you...."

Tanner groaned and tucked her beneath him. He moved his hand between them, finding her, caressing the aching warmth that she pressed boldly against his fingers. "Do you like this?"

"Yes. Yes." Abby felt her breath coming in ragged gasps. She felt sensitized, helpless, limp with ecstasy. He moved away for a moment and rifled through his suitcase and she knew he was protecting her.

"I can't wait, Tanner. Please."

Tanner was over her in seconds, taking her words, her need into his mouth as he rose up and plunged deep inside her. Abby gasped, her legs trembling, her mind gone. His hands moved to her hips, cupping her buttocks, moving inside her at a fevered pitch. With a groan she wrapped her legs around his waist, stirring quakes and tremors and explosive moans from him.

She loved his response to her. She loved him. She arched, moving with him, her hands, her nails finding his back, digging into his skin as her core threatened to erupt.

"I can't hold on," she whispered frantically as waves of pure sensation flashed and flooded within her.

"Don't, sweetheart. Don't." He grew even harder inside her as her body tightened around him. He pounded into her over and over, as stroke after stroke drove her—drove them—fast and frantic over the edge.

Abby cried out, exploding from head to toe. Tanner

growled her name, his back arching, his body shuddering. He grabbed her fiercely as she clung just as tightly to him, release taking them both.

Neither one moved for a moment, catching their breaths, letting the calm pass through them. Moonlight streamed through the window, hitting Tanner on the shoulder. He could barely think, barely wrap his mind around the feelings that were running through him. Never had he felt so out of control. Never had he felt so satisfied. And it bothered him. Hell, it scared him. Without a word he rolled onto his side, taking her with him. He held her tightly against him, feeling possessive and only partly satiated.

"I like you on top of me," she protested, flirting, stealing all tranquility from his body, making him hard and ready once again.

"I don't want to crush you."

She looked up and raised a brow at him. "I'm no wilting flower, Tanner."

"I know," he said, understanding the double meaning whether it was intended or not. She was telling him she understood the future, that she knew what he could and could not offer her.

He smiled, his eyes searching hers. "You amaze me."

"I do?"

"I've never known anyone like you, Abby."

"Is that a good thing?" she asked on a laugh.

He thought about that for a moment. This was all new to him. This cozy, quiet chat, this undeterred feeling of want and need for a woman. "Yes," he said aloud. "Very good. Too good."

She smiled and snuggled closer to him, then pointed to a scar on his shoulder. "Ouch," she whispered, lowering her mouth to the jagged scar and giving it a soft kiss. "How did this happen?"

"I was nine years old. I was going too fast on my bike." He let his hand roam up her leg to her hip.

She pressed into his hand. "Ah, a daredevil. I like that."

He chuckled. "What about you? Any marks on this beautiful body?"

"Nope," she said proudly. "I'm perfect."

His gaze dropped to her breasts. "You certainly are."

She put a finger under his chin and lifted, reestablishing eye contact. "Thank you, sir."

He groaned. "Oh, no. Not that again."

She draped her leg over his. "By the way, what's the C. K. stand for?"

His lips found her ear. "Cute kid."

Tanner could almost feel her smile. "I'll bet," she whispered breathlessly as he seared kisses down her neck.

"Or maybe it was curious kid." His hand moved to her breast, urging the rosy peak into pebble hardness. "I can't remember." He sat back on his knees and lifted the blanket over his head. "Can the questions wait until later?"

Her green eyes sparkled. "How much later?"

He smiled devilishly, then disappeared under the covers, turning Abby's laughter into soft moans.

Eight

"It's 2:00 a.m. Aren't you tired?"

"Not really." In her terry-cloth robe, curled into her spot on the small paisley sofa near the fireplace, Abby glanced up at Tanner and smiled. "Besides, this is the best time of day."

She stared longingly at him, temporarily forgetting her sketchpad, pencil and plans to draw him. He would have done well as an artist's model himself, she mused, taking in the rippled muscles in his back and sleek curve of his firm backside. The soft yellow lamplight cast an amber glow about the room. Tanner lay naked on his stomach on the bed, surrounded by tousled sheets, his chin resting on his palm, his gaze on her, looking too damn sexy for his own good.

She hadn't told Tanner, but she'd turned twenty-five two hours ago. This weekend, this night—it was the best birthday present she could ever ask for.

After they'd made love a second time, Abby hadn't wanted to go to sleep. She didn't want the night to end. Or was it that she didn't want the morning to come? she thought wryly. Either way, she'd grasped on to the surge of energy in her body like a life preserver and acted on her impulse to draw him. He'd balked at the idea at first, but soon gave in when he realized how much it meant to her.

Looking up at her, he dragged a hand through his hair, the movement causing his shoulder and what she could see of his chest muscles to bunch and flex.

She swallowed the lump of desire in her dry throat. "Try to hold still, please."

"Yes, ma'am," he said on a laugh. "I thought an artist needed plenty of sunlight to capture her subject."

"Depends on the subject."

He raised a lazy brow. "Really?"

She nodded. "And the mood she's trying to capture."

"And what mood are you trying to capture, Abby?"

His voice was low and husky, his words sexually baiting, and she watched, hypnotized, as his gaze moved over her.

"A peaceful mood, I guess," she fairly stammered, forcing herself to look down and concentrate on the incomplete sketch that was beginning to take on life. Just like her, she mused. Just like him.

"There's nothing peaceful about my mood," he said tightly.

Her pencil hovered over the paper as she fought for control of her unruly mind and body.

He cleared his throat. "So, why did you decide to become an artist?"

She found herself smiling at that. "Oh, Tanner. No one decides to become an artist. The desire, the drive, the feeling of the brush or pencil in your hand, it all conspires against you. Those elements and many more decide for you, until it becomes an obsession."

He nodded. "Understood. Then perhaps a better question is, why teach it?"

She looked up and sighed. "I love the expression on my students' faces when they've done a good job. The way they sit back and stare at their work and think, 'I did that?'"

"But if you just concentrated on your own painting, you could become wealthy and famous one day."

She brushed her thumb over the paper, working the shading of his calf muscles. "Wealth and fame don't interest me. I grew up in a poor family with hand-me-downs and spaghetti four times a week. I actually liked sharing a room."

"I'm not minding it much myself."

She glanced up at him then, her cheeks burning as hotly as the rest of her, and completely lost her train of thought. "What were we talking about?"

He chuckled, looking pleased with himself. "Your adolescence and how finances never played a role in your family."

"Oh, right." She shrugged. "It's true. I was a

happy child, and I respected my parents for who they were, how much they loved us and how hard they worked.'' She smiled. ''Still do.''

He looked past her for a moment, out the window, and she wondered if he'd ever felt any of those things for anyone. She wondered if wealth and fame were what he respected, loved—what made him happy.

''You'd be content with hand-me-downs and spaghetti, Abby?'' he said at last.

She nodded. ''With the right man, yes.''

His jaw twitched, and her heart dropped. She hadn't meant to go there. She hadn't wanted to talk about family and love and other men and futures without each other.

She tossed her sketchpad and pencil onto the bed and forced her voice to be light. ''Your turn.''

He looked down at the paper, then back up at her, his eyes slowly returning to playful. ''I thought I already had my turn.''

''No, silly.'' She stood up and slipped off her robe. ''It's your turn to draw me.''

Tanner grew hard instantly. She was standing less than ten feet away, looking to the side as she placed one hand across her chest, attempting to look demure. But she didn't. She looked hot and sexy and he wanted her. He gritted his teeth. She was wearing nothing but a smile and she expected him to draw her?

He tried to chuckle, but it came out as more of a choke. ''Abby, I can't—''

''Try not to look at me in a sexual way,'' she suggested.

"Get serious."

She laughed. "I am serious. Start at my foot, but don't see it as a foot. See it, see me, as a series of lines and shapes. Then work your way up." She bent down and touched her heel, then she brushed her fingers up her ankle to her calf. "Curves in, then out, then in again at the back of the knee. But they're all different depths."

"You keep talking like that and I'm taking you right there on that rug," he warned her.

She smiled, her eyes twinkling. "I'll try to use less provocative words."

Tanner scoffed at that. Anything she said, any way she moved, it was all provocative. His gaze raked her as she stood directly in front of the couch. Her toned calves, one lightly muscled thigh draped across the other to hide the sweetness he'd tasted earlier and desperately wanted again. Then there was her flat stomach, extending upward to meet the creamy slopes of her breasts, the rosy nipples just barely hidden by her crossed arm.

He was no artist. He'd never do her justice.

"Just try," she said as if she could read his mind, only barely breaking the spell she cast over him. "Do an outline of my frame."

He shook his head. This was crazy. But hell, he'd been acting crazy since the moment he'd met her. And if he had to tell the truth, he was enjoying it immensely.

With his hand shaking like a damn juvenile delinquent stealing his first glance at a *Playboy* centerfold, he picked up the charcoal pencil and attempted to focus on the lines.

He made it to the outline of her thigh with moderate ease, but he was starting to lose it when he drew the curve of her hip. He almost jumped off the bed and laid her out on that couch when he came to the outline of her breast. But he fought the ache in his groin, the desperate want, and pressed onward, up over her shoulder to the valley of her neck, to her profile. As he drew the lines of her eyes and nose and lips, he wondered if this ache he felt for her would ever go away. When he returned to L.A. would he be able to let her go?

"How's it going?" she asked, tugging him from thoughts and questions he wasn't prepared to answer.

"Rough," he practically growled as his gaze rested on the sketched outline of her nipple. "Real rough."

"Can I see?"

"It'll cost you."

"How much?"

"How much you got?"

She walked over to him, her eyes glowing with passion. "This enough?"

He reached out and hauled her to him, inhaling that scent that he knew he'd never forget. "What perfume do you wear?"

"I don't. It's Ivory soap. Not very sophisticated, huh?"

"It's intoxicating." He turned her around and sat her in his lap. "What do you think of my art?"

He heard her sharp intake of breath as she felt him hard as granite beneath her. "Not bad," she breathed, twisting toward him, pressing him back on the bed. "Not bad at all."

"Not bad for a dying man," he said, tossing the sketchpad aside.

With a seductive smile, she stretched out on top of him. But she didn't stay put for long. Hell-bent on torturing him, she moved slowly down the length of his body, her nipples grazing his chest, his stomach, then over the solid heat of him. "You feel very healthy to me," she whispered as her head lowered and she took him into her mouth.

"Abby." His groan was fierce. Blood pounded in his brain, firing shots of desire so intense it was close to pain. How could she act so coy when he was about to explode? How could she make him see stars, make him want, make him need something he couldn't have?

It was sweet torture, but he wanted her, needed her closer. "Abby, please. I want to kiss you until you're crazy. I want to watch your eyes change color as I bury myself deep inside you."

Her breath caught. "I want that, too." Then she smiled slowly. "But first things first." Like a sweet cat, she moved up, supplying every electric inch of him with kisses. Delicate little kisses, tormenting him beyond reason.

Finally her lips met his. On a growl he took her kiss deep, thrusting his tongue into the heat of her mouth as his big hands cupped her buttocks tightly. Her breath caught and she followed him. And for just a moment he wondered what he'd done to deserve this heaven.

Their mouths warred as their bodies bucked, thrusting toward a paradise they were only just discovering in each other. He lifted her easily, shifting her forward so he could take one soft sloping breast into his mouth.

He felt her shudder, felt the sublime wetness that he'd prompted in her against his belly.

"Sweetheart," he whispered. It was a cry for release, but from what he wasn't exactly sure.

"Yes?" She sighed the word, and it almost did him in.

He had her on her back in a breath, was raised above her in seconds. "For the next several hours I'm giving the lessons."

Her gaze locked with his as she slowly opened her legs. "I'm gonna be a great student."

Longing filled him as he called out her name, as he pushed into the slick channel of her body.

As he pushed home.

That flicker of a thought vanished as she moved beneath him, her hips rising to greet every thrust he gave her.

He was a madman. His movements turned quick and fever-pitched as he pumped inside her. But he would wait to hear her cry out against his mouth.

And when she finally did, when her moans of pleasure turned hot and frantic, he let his mind and body go—go to her—and over the edge of what was real and sound.

To that sweet paradise once again.

Nine

The morning sun spilled through the window, illuminating a small pot of violets on a table across the room. Abby moved her gaze from the sweet, purple flowers to the sexy man sleeping next to her. Of course, she couldn't see Tanner's face. Her cheek rested on his chest, her arm wrapped around his waist, her leg draped over his legs.

She closed her eyes for a moment and let his breathing, let the rise and fall of his chest soothe her. She would allow herself to enjoy this moment—this little slice of heaven—and she wouldn't give in to any feelings of regret for last night or penny wishes that it could continue when they returned to Los Angeles tomorrow.

He was a confirmed bachelor. She knew that without a doubt, she also understood why. He was protecting himself. Hell, if every person *she'd* loved had abandoned her, whether their leaving was deliberate or not, she wouldn't be giving her heart away, either. The word *commitment* was forever taboo in his life's dictionary, and was probably displayed in plain view right underneath the ''L'' word. From all that Jan had told her, he didn't trust people, and no matter how hard she tried to get close to him, he was sure to push her away.

Lord, she didn't want to back him into a corner he wasn't ready for—and perhaps never would be ready for. And she knew she wouldn't be able to stand hearing his words of rejection. Yes, she decided as she lay there, his heart beating softly beneath her cheek, it was better to pretend she didn't love him, pretend that she was more than comfortable being with him for the time that was left. She wouldn't even ask him if they could continue their relationship when they got back to Los Angeles. Instead she'd act as though that was the furthest thing from her mind—when all she really wanted to do was love him.

She stretched, her hand inadvertently traveling up his chest, her thigh sliding upward. She felt him stir, felt his body harden.

''Good morning, my little artist.'' His voice was raspy, sexy and she felt her heart melt like a Popsicle in August.

''Morning,'' she returned simply. ''Tanner, maybe we should—''

''We should,'' he interrupted, nuzzling her neck. ''We definitely should.''

''That's not…ah…well—'' Abby couldn't think or

talk when he was doing that. *Damn him.* How was she going to resist him, much less pretend she didn't love him?

His hand grazed her inner thigh and she sighed. Later. She'd resist him later.

Tanner came up on one elbow and looked deep into Abby's eyes, the green orbs flecked with heat. She shocked the hell out of him. Well, his feelings for her did, anyway. Never in his life had a woman affected him like this. Awake, asleep, posing for him, lying beneath him, she made him think about things that he thought he'd never feel, things he thought he'd never want. In the road map of his life, he hadn't seen a picture of Abby. But here she was. A curve in the road, a detour, a stop sign. He hadn't seen her coming.

From age seven his future had made sense. It was comfortable, even if it wasn't ideal. With his father jet-setting from one exotic locale to the next, Tanner had been on his own after his grandmother died. He went straight into boarding school, came out at sixteen, went to college, made a million by twenty-three. He'd spent a lifetime proving he didn't need anyone or anything.

Last night had changed that. No. Abby had changed that.

He smiled as she, too, rose up on one elbow, her red hair falling about her shoulders, her creamy skin aching for his touch. "Sun's shining. It looks like it's going to be a beautiful day."

Damned beautiful. He pulled her close. She responded immediately, wrapping her arms around his neck. Tanner felt any last shreds of control slipping away as he captured her mouth hungrily. Why couldn't he have his cake and eat it, too? Marriage wasn't in his future, but continuing to see Abby when they returned to L.A. certainly could be.

She rolled on top of him, her eyes already dark with passion. She gasped, then smiled when she found him hard and ready for her. "I must warn you, I'm not getting out of this bed until I'm satisfied."

Tanner couldn't help but smile. "That's a serious threat. What happens if I won't deliver?"

"Won't or can't?" she teased, rubbing her breasts seductively against his chest.

Tanner sucked in his breath. "Oh, sweetheart. You have no idea what you're in for."

She gave him a half smile. "I'm more than willing to find out."

"Then hold on."

She did. And in one quick movement he lifted her up and placed her down on top of him. She cried out, then began to move, drawing him in and out of her. His body bucked and his mind reeled and took flight from a truth he didn't recognize as his gaze caught the erotic sight of their shadows on the wall.

It was close to ten when they were finally up and fairly ready. Abby sat on the edge of the bed and took a bite of one of the pumpkin muffins that had mysteriously appeared, along with some fresh bacon and hot coffee, outside the guest-house door. A soft knock and departing footsteps were all the clues they'd had, but she was willing to bet her bottom dollar that Jan was behind the breakfast.

"You've inspired me," Tanner announced suddenly, pulling on his jeans.

"I know. You told me." Already dressed, Abby just sat back and admired him. "Several times last night and a couple of times this morning."

He arched a brow at her. "Oh, sweetheart, this is a different kind of inspiration altogether."

Did a more handsome man even exist? she wondered as she watched him pull a tan sweater over his head. The color turned his eyes dark chocolate and his skin bronze. With his hiking boots and baseball cap he looked rugged, still powerful, but outdoorsy. He was just irresistible and she knew when she returned to work tomorrow afternoon, she was going to have to put in her two-week notice. The thought ripped at her heart, but there was no way she could see him every day, work so close to him and yet be so far away. Hell, Greenland would be too close.

Tanner leaned against the wall, sporting a cocky grin. "I have the perfect concept for our signature sweet."

"Well, out with it, man," she demanded playfully. "Don't make me torture you."

"Damn, that sounds tempting." He walked over and grabbed her hand. "But we don't have much time. Come with me."

They were out the door, past the lake and running toward the orchard before Tanner slowed. Apple trees surrounded them when he finally stopped.

"This is the Tanner signature sweet?" Abby said, slightly out of breath. "An orchard?"

"Yes."

Abby looked around, the delicate fragrance of apple tickling her senses. This spot was like a dream come true for her. Picture perfect, and for just a moment she wished she could hold an art class here. Under the pale-blue sky, resting amongst orange and red and yellowed maple leaves that had blown here on the wind, then scattered about, were hundreds of apple trees. Apples hung daintily off branches, thick trunks were carved with age and experience. The trees looked ready to climb, ready for harvesting. And Abby wondered why she hadn't come here before, but felt happy that Tanner had discovered it.

She turned back to face him, and found him looking far too smug for his own good. He needed a woman to bring him down a peg or two. But it wouldn't be her, she knew, and that thought made a lump the size of a grapefruit form in her throat. She forced herself to swallow. "So, you're going to cover an apple tree in marshmallows?"

He grinned at her. "Not the tree, smart-aleck. And we're not going to use marshmallows. We're going to create the most scrumptious, amazing chocolate-nut apple ever."

"No more working separately, then?" She smiled a little shyly. "What I meant was—"

"I know what you meant." His voice turned low and husky and he came to stand before her. "Coming together sounds so much better, don't you think?"

Oh, did it ever. She nodded, trying to ignore the

heat that emanated from him and landed deep in her belly. "Yes. I think so. Yes."

Amusement burned brightly behind his eyes. He knew his effect on her and he obviously reveled in it. "I'm going to name it the Abby Apple."

"A sweet named after me? That's a lot of pressure." She tried not to drown in this playful side of him, but she felt herself slipping beneath the surface. "People will expect me to be sweet all the time."

"That's not much of a stretch." He snaked an arm around her waist, pulled her close and planted a kiss on her open mouth. He groaned and whispered, "So sweet."

She longed for him to pick her up and carry her off to his lair—or the guest house—as he had last night, but she needed to at least make some attempt at playing it cool and calm. "I still don't understand the inspiration part."

He released her and gestured around. "The apple tree. You told me about it that first night at dinner. You said you wanted one."

"You remember that?"

He raised a brow. So proud, so self-assured, he'd probably memorized her life story. Lord, did she love that. She loved him. "When do we get started?"

"Now." Tanner picked a few apples off the tree and tossed them to her. "We have to present our sample at dinner tonight."

"Something's missing."

"Is that so?" Tanner grinned at Abby. Standing next to him at the stove, she nibbled on his invention—a damned good-looking chocolate-and-walnut-covered apple—and wore a thoughtful expression. She looked cute in her apron—chocolate and powdered sugar staining her cheek and jaw. "What would you suggest, Chef Tell?"

"Don't get me wrong," she began. "This is delicious and...what was the other word you used? Scrumptious." She continued to stir the warm chocolate. "I just think it needs an extra touch."

He shot her a look of warning. "No marshmallows."

She laughed. "I think that was ruled out after my last candy-making attempt. How about caramel? Before we dip the apple in chocolate, let's dip it in caramel."

"That might be too much for the palate to take."

Abby handed him a bag of caramels. "You sound like a real candy company owner now. If I didn't know why you really wanted this company, I'd think you were striving to be Willy Wonka."

"Maybe I am," he said quickly. "Maybe this just isn't about acquisitions anymore." Willy Wonka. He'd have to rent that movie when he returned home. Abby hadn't seen his screening room. Maybe they could watch it together. They could make popcorn, talk about new ideas for the company, snuggle on the couch. Then he could take her up to his bedroom and make love to her all night.

Tanner's cell phone rang, interrupting his impossible fantasy, while reminding him that his life really was about acquisitions and transactions. He glanced at the number. The office. It was Jeff.

"I'm all right in here," Abby said, melting the caramel over a low flame. "Got everything under control if you want to take that outside."

Tanner paused. For the first time in his life he felt happy, a bottomless sense of peace, and he wasn't about to interrupt that today. So, for the first time in his life, he ignored the call, punching the power button ruthlessly even while it continued to ring.

Whatever Jeff had to tell him could wait until later, he decided, watching Abby dip the apples into the hot caramel. Then she took a cooled one and dipped it in the chocolate. She was gentle and absorbed and she impressed the hell out of him.

He stifled a laugh at the thought of any of the women he'd dated making candy, wearing a T-shirt and jeans and very little makeup, wanting to be more than a trophy on his arm.

Tanner sidled up behind Abby and put his arms around her waist. Her perfume, that Ivory soap scent that made him wild, wafted delicately from her skin. She felt so good to him. "I'm not taking any calls. I'm working here today. With you."

She hesitated, then glanced over her shoulder at him. "Well, since you've bagged all outside business and since you're a nut yourself, I think it only fitting that you get to roll the Abby Apple in the walnuts."

He chuckled, gave her a squeeze and then released her. He tossed his phone onto the counter and took his position in front of the walnut area that Abby had set up.

They worked side by side, a two-person assembly line, talking, making stupid jokes, tossing specks of powdered sugar at each other. But the best part was when Abby would pass him an apple, and her small, delicate fingers would touch his for just a moment.

To a man like him, such a small gesture should hardly count as foreplay. It was lingering and coy and childish. But with her, it was pure sensuality.

"Oh, man," he said a moment later, after cutting into one apple and popping a slice into his mouth. "This is...you have to taste this."

Tanner brought the slice of apple up to her mouth. Her eyes locked with his as she took a bite.

"Good," she breathed, nodding excitedly. "So good."

She made the mistake of running her tongue over her lower lip, her eyes magnetic. She should be painted like this, Tanner mused, fighting the urge to pitch the apple and fill his hand with something soft and sweet instead. But he'd made plans for them this afternoon. Plans that couldn't be blown off.

His jaw tight, he looked away. "Let's leave the rest to cool." His tone was practically a growl as he led her out the laboratory door. "While you were in the shower, I arranged a little surprise for you."

"I'm not going." Fear shot into Abby's chest as she looked around the airplane hangar, trying not to focus on the small white plane that was trailing an even smaller white plane behind it. For God's sake, which one was he expecting her to board? The smallest one looked like it had roller skates for wheels. "I can barely get on a big jet, much less this little two-seater thing."

Tanner put a reassuring arm around her shoulders and pointed to the larger of the two planes—which wasn't saying much. "That's a Piper Supercub, and attached to the back is a glider. There's no motor. We glide on the wind."

"That's a confidence builder," she muttered.

"That's exactly what I'm trying to give you. Confidence. You've got to run straight through your fear."

"Why?"

He turned her to face him. "Fear holds you hostage for the rest of your life, Abby. That's no way to live."

She attempted to crack a smile. "It's been working fine for me so far."

"I'll be right with you. Helping you."

"Helping *me?*" she cried. "Helping me what?"

He crossed his arms over his chest, his expression smug, as if he'd just split the atom. "You're going to do the navigating. Of course, I'll help you. There are elevator controls in both the front and the back of the glider, so we'll be doing it together."

"I don't have a license or—" she sputtered.

"You don't have to have a license to move the controls as long as a licensed pilot's sitting behind you." He grinned. "And I will be."

Abby felt her mouth fall open and her heart sink into her shoes. "You're crazy."

"I'll be there backing you up if there are any problems."

"If?" she practically squeaked.

"I have two gliders back in California. I soar all

the time, and I have hundreds of hours of flight experience.''

"Perfect. Then you can take yourself for a drive. I'll watch from down here. Safe. In one piece. On the ground.''

Tanner took her hands in his, his eyes staring straight into her soul. "Do something for me?''

"What's that?''

"Trust me.'' He squeezed her hands. "I won't let you get hurt.''

Too late for that, she thought, and she wasn't talking about the glider. Tomorrow her heart would be broken and she'd have only memories and a shaky sketch of the man of her dreams. She looked away, looked down, looked anywhere but in his eyes. She didn't want to be afraid anymore. Of flying or of falling in love. She'd dived into one as blind as all get-out, so why not the other?

"What makes you think I can do this?'' she asked him.

"I believe in you. Simple as that.''

"And I suppose you don't do that very often?''

He winked at her. "You'd be supposing right.''

He believed in her. In her wildest dreams she'd never imagined a man saying such a thing to her. Especially this man. And, she realized, that gave her courage. She swallowed hard. "Well, what are we waiting for? Let's board this spacecraft.''

"Aircraft,'' Tanner corrected on a chuckle.

An older man wearing a leather jacket with the airfield's insignia on it—who Abby could only presume was the pilot of the Piper—came over to check on them. "You and your wife ready to go, sir?"

Tanner raised a brow at Abby. "Are we?"

Ignoring the terrible tenseness overtaking her, Abby felt herself nod. "Ready as I'll ever be."

Adrift on air. Pure sunlight, breathless peace. A silent orchestra played the music of the clouds, the blue, the vastness. Tanner had been right, Abby realized. Sweet, fragrant air rushed over her face through the small ventilator to her left. All around her the countryside looked small and lush. If she had allowed fear to guide her decision, she never would have felt such deliciousness.

At her hand, her will, the glider curved, then evened out. Her stomach dipped, then relaxed. From behind her Tanner chuckled and said the "Excellent," and she felt proud.

Of course, she hadn't become a steady-handed convert immediately. No. At first, when she'd climbed into the glider's small bucket seat and the Piper had taken off down the runway, she'd pretended to be brave. Sweat had broken out pretty much everywhere as they'd soared up, up and around, into the sky, up to regulation height. But terror had truly gripped her heart when Tanner unhooked the cable that connected them to the Piper and let them go—let them ride on the wind, as he'd said from behind her.

Abby's first thoughts had come in a jumbled panic. No motor? Absolute silence but for the departing Piper. Tanner expected her to steer this thing? Where were they going to land? Had he plotted all this out?

But in seconds he was showing her how to move with the air currents, how to find the thermals that would carry them for miles. Then something amazing had happened. One instant she felt out of control, the next she felt in control, at ease, confident. And she'd let herself go, hearing his instruction and his praise distinctly over the gentle breeze.

Pure heaven.

"Are you okay?" Tanner called.

"Wonderful," she answered, pushing a strand of hair out of her face, hooking it behind her ear.

"Then happy birthday, Abby."

She gasped. "How did you—"

"I have my spies," he said. "So what do you think? Good present or bad present?"

Abby took in the beauty from above and felt tears come to her eyes. "Really good present. It's amazing up here."

"There's nothing like your first time."

"It's so different." She marveled at the awe in her own voice. "So uncomplicated and peaceful. Like a calm sea."

"Curve just a little to the right," he instructed, and she could feel him moving his controls along with her. "We have to stay in the thermal."

Once they were steady, Abby settled farther into her seat. "The air's so clear up here."

Tanner chuckled. "No L.A. smog in the Minnesota sky. Look down there. To your left."

She did as he asked, gasping as she saw deer, fifty or so, running through the trees, almost following the direction of the glider.

"And you have two of these?" She laughed, amazed, envious. "Do you fly over the ocean back home?"

"No, the air's better in mountain ranges. I fly out in Warner Springs. Sunset's the best time."

"Oh, I'd love that," she said quietly, almost to herself.

But he'd heard her. "You're welcome to join me. Anytime."

Tension and want and hope knotted in her stomach. Had he asked her to see him again or was he just being gracious? she wondered as a mild gust of wind sent the glider upward, fast and smooth. No doubt it was the latter.

"How long have you been interested in flying?" she asked him, her tone just a trace unsteady.

"Seems like forever. My grandmother was an exceptional pilot. She was the one who introduced me to flying. Her bookcases were stacked with manuals and biographies of famous pilots. I suppose she passed her obsession on to me."

"Did she take you up in a glider or a plane?"

"Neither. She died before we had a chance to fly together."

Abby was thoughtful for a moment as they sailed through a patch of low clouds. "Tanner?"

"Yeah?"

"This high up, we're pretty close to heaven. I'd say your grandmother has probably flown with you more times than you think."

He didn't say anything and she fought the urge to turn around and look at him. Instead, she opted for changing the subject. "When I was a kid, I used to take my dollhouse outside and put it on the lawn. I even laid out the landscaping stuff like trees and rocks and things. Then I'd climb up on my roof and look out at my miniature setting. I felt like a giant. 'Course, it didn't look as small as down there, but the same idea."

"I can't believe you went onto the roof. I thought you were afraid of heights."

"No, I wasn't afraid of anything back then." She was quiet for a moment, then she sighed. "The roof always felt so magical to me. It was easy to get to from my bedroom window. Just up the tree and you're there." She smiled in remembrance. "Sure I fell off a couple times, but hey, it was my special place."

He snorted. "The boys know how easy it was to get up to your room with the help of that tree?"

"I didn't have many boyfriends in school."

"I don't believe it."

"Well, it's true," she said, breathing in the scents of sun and earth and cool that seemed to change in potency every few minutes. "I was the poor girl in a rich community. My father's an amazing carpenter, and my mom wanted to stay home with us. So we had lots of love, but not much money. The kids at school didn't really notice me, unless it was to call me names and make fun of my family."

"Immaturity breeds stupidity," Tanner said simply.

"What about you? I bet you had all the girls fighting over you in school."

He laughed. "I went to a boys' academy. There wasn't much chance to date and certainly no place to take them."

"Well," she said, gazing out over the rolling hills and curving ponds. "This would be it. The perfect place to bring a woman." She hesitated. "I'm sure they're all really impressed when you take them up here."

"I've never brought a woman up into the sky before."

A hush fell. Just the gentle breeze and the faint sound of her pulse racing could be heard at his welcome admission. She didn't reply, she didn't want this moment, this memory, to be ruined. She merely smiled and poured her focus back into the leisurely journey, into the beautiful panoramic vision of autumn.

Ten

"**Y**our bath has been drawn, Your Highness." Tanner smiled as he held the bathroom door open for Abby.

They'd returned from their flying adventure just a little while ago, after a shaky descent but a perfect landing—onto a long stretch of pastureland. Clouds had been moving over the sun by the time Tanner and Abby were brought back to the airport by one of the ground crew. But before they'd gotten into the limo, Tanner hadn't been able to stop himself from gathering her in his arms for just a moment, brushing a kiss on her soft lips. He'd never felt so proud of anyone in his life.

On their ride home she'd mentioned that the tension from conquering her fear had made her tired and her muscles sore. And though Tanner wanted nothing more than to give her an all-over body massage, he knew that wouldn't be wise. A bath was much better, safer, when they only had thirty minutes until dinner.

He'd showered and dressed already, leaving the bathroom for her.

"Come on. Your bath's getting cold, birthday girl," he called with halfhearted impatience.

She emerged from the walk-in closet like an angel. A cloud of red curls, white bathrobe and bare feet. "Are there bubbles?"

He harrumphed, forcing back his desire. "Are there bubbles? It's like the inside of a champagne bottle in that tub."

"Very good," she said with a sassy smile, coming to stand before him. "For your hard work and—" she ran her hand up the lapel of his charcoal suit "—because you look really, really sexy, you shall be granted one wish."

"Only one?"

"Don't press your luck."

He put both hands up in submission. "All right, all right. Let me think a moment." He rubbed his chin pensively, his thoughts traveling from one seductive image of Abby to the next. Until…

"I've got it," he announced.

"What is your wish, sir?"

He leaned back against the doorjamb and crossed his arms over his chest. "I request that you leave the bathroom door ajar."

First her eyes widened, then she laughed, her cheeks flushing a pretty pink. "To what end?"

Slipping a finger into the loose knot at her waist,

he eased the ties of her robe free. "So your humble servant may peek in and watch you bathe this time."

"This time?" She sighed, her eyes filling with passion as his hands found her waist, then raked up her back and down her hips.

A fire raged inside him, and he knew if he didn't stop touching her this very minute they were going to miss their candy presentation, dinner and maybe breakfast, as well. He took her hands in his. "Last time you had a bath, I was forced to stay outside the door with only my imagination to keep me company.

She grinned. "That wasn't very fair of me." She moved closer to him. Through the thin robe the tips of her breasts met with his shirt, his chest. "And as I am a very fair person, your wish is granted."

Red-hot desire flooded his senses and he involuntarily squeezed her hand, feeling his grandmother's ring beneath his palm.

She squeezed back. "I had a good time today, Tanner. Floating on air. It was the best birthday present I've ever been given. Thank you."

"It was my pleasure," he returned, his voice hoarse, his body electrified. Would he ever get enough of her? "I meant it when I said anytime."

She nodded. "It would be wonderful if I could."

He felt his brow lift. "And why couldn't you?"

She shrugged and looked away from him. "I don't know that I'll have much time for…socializing when I get back home."

He chuckled. "Well, maybe I can tear you away from that art class for a quick dinner, then."

"Maybe." Her gaze flickered toward him, her

mouth turning up into a half smile. "If I can find the time."

If I can find the time? He knew that she was kidding, but even the thought of not seeing her, not being close to her, made his blood turn cold. He swept her into his arms and lowered his mouth to hers.

She was quick to respond, moaning as her fingers plunged into his hair. He thrust his tongue into her mouth and she met him, drawing him further, deeper. Damn, how he wanted her.

She loved his kiss and she wanted more, he knew, and that knowledge threatened to send him over the edge, threatened to make them late—very late.

"Tanner." She sighed, melting against him, her robe slipping off her shoulders, baring one beautiful breast to his burning gaze.

He surrendered. He was her slave for as long as she wanted him, he vowed, his gaze fixated longingly on the taut peak, swollen and waiting, driving him mad. Abby's head fell back, encouraging him, and he complied, taking the dusky nipple into his mouth, teasing, caressing with his tongue. There was no other way to describe how he felt with her, the effect she had over him. It was unnatural, yet to Tanner there was nothing more natural in the world.

"Are you sure?" he whispered against her breast.

"About what?" she queried hoarsely.

He trailed hot kisses up her neck to her mouth. "Are you sure you don't have the time for me?"

She hesitated, then looked up at him, her eyes a glassy haze of want and need. "You're right. We don't want to be late for dinner."

Tanner groaned, ready to kick himself. He'd meant did she have the time for him when they got back to L.A. With every ounce of control he had left, he slipped her robe back up over her shoulders, then gave her a quick kiss on the lips. "You get in that tub, princess." He raised a brow. "And don't forget about the door."

She tried to look imperious. "Do you know what happens when you make demands of your monarch?"

He grinned devilishly. "I'm sentenced to forty days in her bed?"

"Don't forget about the forty nights." She laughed and disappeared into the steamy bathroom, leaving the door ajar—and leaving Tanner with a volatile sense of longing. He stared at the open doorway, waiting, his jaw as tight as his groin.

When she reached the foot of the tub, she turned, gave him a smile and slipped off her robe. He snaked in a breath as she stepped into the water and slowly sank into the bath. After a moment she stood and reached for a sponge on the counter. She caught his gaze and smiled again. His mouth went bone dry. Soapsuds clung to her glistening skin, barely covering the intimate areas of her. She stood like that for a long moment, letting him admire her before she slipped back beneath the water and began to run the sponge sensuously over her arms and long, graceful neck.

He'd like to draw her like that, he mused, making a silent vow to explore every inch of her again and again, later in their bed when nothing could interrupt them.

* * *

"Left foot red," Jan called.

With pure affection, Abby watched the pink-cheeked woman and her husband pop two more slices of the Abby Apple—which had been deemed a hit by everyone—into their mouths as they pointed and laughed at the Twister players.

To Abby's surprise, dinner had been more than civilized. All the other "contestants" who were hoping to purchase Swanson Sweets were agreeable and affable, and no one discussed business. Instead they told stories, shared what they'd done that day and bragged about their kids.

Soon after nine, the other two couples left, claiming they had a long drive or a late flight. It was clear to everyone that the Swansons considered Abby and Tanner family. And to Abby that knowledge brought her pleasure as well as sadness for having lied to them. Jan knew their secret, of course, but Abby wondered if the woman had told her husband. Would Frank still want Tanner to have his company if he knew the truth? Hopefully, Tanner would do well by the company, parent it the way she knew he could, so that in some small way he would be making Frank and Jan proud.

They *had* looked proud when she and Tanner had presented the Abby Apple after the delicious meal of roast beef and garlic mashed potatoes. They even went so far as to say they wished to talk to Abby and Tanner later, complete with a wink from Jan. Then the older couple announced that there would be no sitting in the parlor drinking coffee and showing off good manners. The Swansons were a game-playing family and all were required to participate. As competitor or cheerleader, you just had to give it your all.

Before he could protest, Tanner was roped into the body-contorting game of Twister—with an amusing hitch attached. Each adult had to carry a child on his shoulders. At first Tanner had looked dazed and confused when Kat put her little girl up on his shoulders. Clearly, he was not used to being around children, and Abby wondered if he was going to beg off. But after a few minutes and with the help of Abby's and the other ladies' enthusiastic cheering, he started to relax and have fun.

Now as Abby sat on the living-room rug between Kat and her sister, Cindy, she watched the game transform from friendly competition into an out-and-out battle for the Twister championship. Everyone was laughing, cheering, twisting, but Tanner and Kat's daughter appeared determined to win.

"Left hand green," Jan called loudly, from her judge's chair behind the cheering section.

"Hey, Abby," Kat said conspiratorially. "My daughter and your husband are whipping the others."

Abby laughed. "I couldn't be more proud."

Kat looked around. "Who wants to put some money on this?"

Cindy gave her an appalled look. "Are you going to bet against your own nephew, not to mention your husband?"

"Do you think they'll forgive me?" Kat asked impishly.

"Not likely." Cindy smiled and nodded at Abby.

"Abby knows how to play it. Supporting her husband."

Abby laughed and Kat snorted. "Give the girl a break. She doesn't know any better. She's still on her honeymoon."

Just then Tanner glanced up and smiled. Abby felt her pulse speed up. With his tie off and his collar unbuttoned, he looked tousled and sexy. He looked so right with a child and she wondered if he'd ever thought about having one.

"Right foot blue," Jan called.

Tanner lifted his leg over Kat's husband's hand, while the little girl on his shoulders held on tight, giggling as she shifted around. Abby couldn't help herself. She cheered and clapped for them.

"Oh, the mooning stage," Kat said good-naturedly. "I loved that stage."

Abby raised her brow. "You don't moon over each other anymore?"

Cindy grunted. "Oh, don't let her fool you."

Kat nodded. "It's different now—better. We know each other's hearts inside and out. That's truly sexy."

"Are you watching these moves?" Tanner called to Abby, flexing his free arm before he put it down on a yellow circle. He winked at her. "Impressed?"

She laughed. "Are you showing off for the ladies?"

He gave her one of his irresistible smiles. "One in particular."

"He really is so adorable, Abby," Cindy said.

Abby smiled and rolled her eyes. "He's a handful."

"Wait until you have kids," Kat said knowingly. "That's a handful."

Cindy raised a brow. "Looks like Tanner's ready for a little one."

Abby looked up just in time to see all but one couple crash down on the Twister mat.

Jan pointed and smiled at Tanner. "The winners," she said gaily. "And what do we have for them, Frank?"

"Chocolate. What else?" Frank said with a wide grin.

Everyone broke out into laughter and began to disperse, offering condolences to the other teams. But Abby couldn't take her eyes off Tanner. She felt her heart warm when he lifted the little girl off his shoulders, turned her around in his arms and gave her a kiss on the cheek. Butterflies fluttered in her stomach, the pink-and-blue kind. The kind only a woman in love can have when she sees her man holding a child.

She couldn't help remembering back to the first time they'd really talked in his house, at his dinner table. Tanner had been charming and suave and sexy, but there had been a decided hardness behind his eyes. He'd lived a cheerless life whether he wanted to admit it or not. Losing everyone who was important and pretending it didn't matter took a lot out of a person.

But in just these past days he'd changed immensely. He'd allowed himself to have fun, make mistakes—become part of a real family. It made her wonder if he had changed his mind and was interested in having a family of his own, or at the very least working toward one.

She watched him give Kat's daughter a congratulatory high-five and thought that nothing in the world would make her happier than to go home tomorrow knowing that she and Tanner had a future. Together.

Tanner lit a match and touched it to the crumpled newspaper under the firewood. The dry timber sparked to life instantly, just the way *he* did when Abby was near. Everything seemed better when she was near, he decided, thinking back over the weekend, even tonight.

Dinner had been enjoyable and successful, with a perfect ending to boot.

Signed contracts.

Frank and Jan had put them in his hand and told him and Abby how happy they were that such wonderful people were buying their company and they had high hopes for a lasting friendship through the years.

A lasting friendship. For some reason those words had stuck with him, filling him with longing.

For the hundredth time since they'd come back to the guest house, he glanced toward the closet, then brushed all thoughts but one from his mind.

Abby. And the night ahead, and waking up with her. But he couldn't have either until she emerged from the closet.

"Abby?"

"Just a sec." He heard rustling and then the closet door opened.

Tanner's jaw dropped. Abby stood there, looking absolutely mind-blowingly beautiful in a creamy-white negligee. Her eyes sparkled, her hair hung loose about her shoulders, and as she leaned against the door like a vamp, several red curls danced straight into the valley between her breasts. Was this the same Abby who'd walked into his office that day, spilling coffee all over his desk? He was reminded of a story he'd read in school about a goddess who could render a man speechless with her beauty.

"Ready to celebrate?" Her voice was low and inviting, and he could just make out her Ivory soap scent.

His hands ached to touch her, but he'd be sure to leave her nightie on as he teased her, tasted her, as he lifted the smooth silky fabric up, up over her hips until he found paradise.

He let his gaze roam the length of her once more. "You look so beautiful."

She went to him and kneeled down next to him. Slowly she took his hand and put it on her breast. "Thank you."

All self-control lost, he pulled her into his lap, his mouth claiming hers, a fire raging in him. She tasted so amazing, like sweet mint. He dragged his lips away for a moment, looking at her. Her eyes were hot and searching, her lips wet and swollen from his kiss.

"This time, here with you, has been so wonderful," she said, her eyes wide and sincere.

Suddenly he felt as though he had to be sure of her. "Abby," he said, choosing his words carefully. "When we get back, I want us to…continue this."

Her eyes widened, those perfect, full, inviting lips parting a fraction. "Tanner, what are you saying?"

Tanner hesitated. She had that look of hopefulness in her eyes, the one he'd seen before when he'd let things go too far. Marriage was not an option, but seeing her again—and often—certainly was. He just needed to find the best way to say that without hurting her.

He cupped her face. "Abby, I—"

A knock at the door made Abby jump and brought a groan to Tanner's lips.

"Maybe Frank and Jan are dropping off some champagne," she suggested, coming to her feet. "You get it. I'll go get some candles from the bathroom." She stood up. "We need to set the proper mood in here."

Tanner stood up. Abby's question was resting heavily on his mind and he wasn't in the mood to entertain. If it was the Swansons bringing champagne, he was going to give them the quickest thank-you in history.

He flung open the door, and like a splash of cold water in the face, he saw Jeff Rhodes standing on the porch with an armful of files and an expectant smile.

"Hi, boss."

"You want to tell me what the hell you're doing here?" Tanner stepped out onto the porch, closing the door to the guest house behind him. The cool night air swept over him as he stared down at his CFO. "This isn't a good time."

Jeff grinned. "I understand." Then he grew serious. "I've been trying to get you on your cell phone all day. When I couldn't get a hold of you, I took the first flight out."

"What's the problem?"

"Harrison's real anxious to take out the competition. He says that he's willing to meet our price for Swanson Sweets, but he wants it finalized in a meeting we've set up for 10:00 a.m. tomorrow."

"Willing to meet our price? Meeting? What are you talking about? I never told you to move forward on the deal with Harrison."

Jeff peered at him closely. "You told me to do my usual song and dance. I'm the CFO. The only song and dance I know is negotiating lucrative deals for Tanner Enterprises."

Tanner's mind went into hyperdrive. That was exactly what he'd told Jeff to do a few days ago. It's what he probably would have done himself. But dammit, now there was more to this deal with Swanson than he'd anticipated. It had become personal, whether he wanted it that way or not.

"You did sign with Swanson, didn't you?" Jeff asked.

Tanner nodded absently, his mind sifting through the conversations and events of the past few days. He'd known that this was a possibility, but it was something he'd planned to deal with—and decide about—when he got home. The preliminary deal he'd discussed with Harrison last month was very profitable, but was by no means finalized. And, he realized with a start, with everything that had been happening, he'd almost forgotten all about it.

"I didn't authorize you to discuss a final deal," Tanner said to Jeff.

"Well, I assumed—"

"Don't ever assume."

Tanner raked a hand through his hair. A week ago he would've been a fool to turn down a deal with

Harrison. But now he wasn't at all sure he wanted to sell. He realized with a jolt that the thrill of the hunt and kill was gone. In its place was a hunger for something more, something lasting.

He walked to the edge of the porch and looked out at the lake. "I don't know if I want to go that way anymore."

"Excuse me?" Jeff said blankly.

"I might keep Swanson Sweets in the family."

"In the family? What family?" Jeff's voice rose slightly on each word. "Who the hell are you?"

Tanner turned and eyed his friend. And friends they were, but this was business, and Jeff did have a tendency to overstep from time to time. "You got something to say to me, Jeff?"

Jeff shrugged. "Plainly speaking, you're acting strange, pal. Where's that hard-ass shark who thrives on killing the competition? We all stand to gain from this deal. It's important." His gaze fell an inch. "I'm just concerned that you've lost your edge."

"You wanna have a go right now?" Tanner countered, his jaw twitching, his pride pushing him into reckless territory. "I'd be happy to show you just how on the ball I am."

Frowning, Jeff shook his head. "I've never seen you like this." He studied his boss for a moment, then his gaze flickered over Tanner's shoulder to the door of the cabin. He let out an incredulous little laugh. "Don't tell me you've fallen in love with the mail girl?"

Tanner narrowed his eyes. "If you ever call her that again, I'll break you in half."

"Fine." Jeff stuffed the files into his briefcase. "I'll go back to L.A., call Harrison and tell him tomorrow morning's meeting is canceled. That'll give his lawyers twelve hours to review the faxes, e-mails and phone messages from Tanner Enterprises to see if they constitute a breach of good faith.''

''Harrison doesn't want to tangle with me,'' Tanner countered. ''Trust me. He knows the power behind Tanner Enterprises.'' And I know it, Tanner thought, remembering how hard he'd worked to achieve a reputation that granted him that kind of power in the world of business. He was successful.

Or was he?

He froze, his mind churning. His one goal in life had always been to be successful. At all costs, of course. Never had being the good guy or the straight-laced businessman been in his plans, and his life had been working just fine—before he'd come here, that is. Before he'd met Abby.

Dammit, what the hell was he doing? Where had his quick, logical thinking gone? Was he really about to back away from a six-million-dollar deal—jeopardize his reputation in the business world—which was essentially the only thing he had, the only thing he could really count on—because he felt all warm and fuzzy for a few days?

He raked a hand through his hair. Abby was wonderful, amazing, but she was temporary, like every other person who'd ever come into his life. That same life that had already proven to him where he belonged and what he was good for. Making deals, not making friends.

Suddenly he had the impression he'd been sleep-walking for three days. And it was time to wake up. He knew what he had to do. The only thing he could do—the only thing that made any sense.

He regarded Jeff with a hard stare. "I'll be back in the office by sunup. Go back tonight and draw up the deal points. I'll finish this myself." He didn't wait to see Jeff leave, he simply turned and walked back across the porch.

When Tanner entered the guest house, he knew he was a different person than when he'd left only moments ago. Gone was the relaxation, the happiness, the freedom.

He saw Abby bundled in her robe, sitting by the fire with her back to him, and he felt himself soften. What *had* happened to him this weekend? Just the sight of her was enough to melt him where he stood.

"I'm sorry about that," he began. "It was my—"

"I know who it was," she said, her tone cool.

He came to sit in front of her, his back to the fire, his heart filling with apprehension. "What's wrong?"

"It was you who left the door open a crack this time, Tanner." She looked up at him, her green eyes penetrating his very soul. "How could you?"

"How could I what?" he asked, and heard the defensiveness in his own voice.

"How can you sell off the Swansons' company the minute you take possession of it? And to a man who's only going to destroy it?"

"It's a hell of a lot of money, Abby. I don't think you understand—"

"You're right about that. I don't understand. I don't get how you could let the Swansons like you and believe in you, trust that you're going to do the best thing for their company, then betray them. Can you explain that to me?"

His jaw twitched. "It's business."

"That's your justification for hurting people?" She

searched his eyes. "I thought you'd changed. I thought you and I were—" She shook her head. "Lord, I don't know what I thought."

Abby's heart kicked painfully. This was not the night she'd imagined—a beautiful night of holding each other, making love and celebrating winning the contest together. It wasn't as though he'd lied to her exactly. But never in her wildest dreams would she have thought that Tanner was going to sell off Swanson Sweets. It was the act of a cold, hard businessman, not the tender, loving man who had held her in his arms last night.

She knew that man still existed somewhere inside him, and she was going to do her best to try to find him even if it meant laying her heart bare. She tried to keep her voice cool and steady. "I fell in love with you, Tanner. Or the man I thought you were."

"Love?" He raked a hand through his hair, his expression restless and detached. "I've told you. I'm not the marrying kind, Abby. I've got a definite need for freedom."

"And that makes me what? A prison?" She stared into the fire. "Marriage isn't about imprisonment. I wanted to be your lover and your friend. I wanted to help you make the right decisions, be there for you when you're sad, tell you off when you're being a jerk."

He exhaled heavily and touched her cheek, turning her to face him. "Abby, I don't want to stop seeing you."

"Maybe that's true today, tomorrow, maybe even a month from now. But strings, ties that bind, they're important to me."

He dropped his hand from her face, his eyes growing cold. "There are no guarantees in life, Abby. People can become lost to you whether they make promises or not."

"So don't get involved, don't care about someone because you're afraid they'll leave you?"

"You got it all wrong, Abby."

"I don't think so." Abby's eye caught sight of her sketchpad peeking out from underneath the bed, and memories of their wonderful night together flooded her mind. She tried again to reach him, his heart. "You know, someone once told me that you have to run through your fear, that living in fear is no life at all."

"What idiot told you that?"

"You did."

He crossed his arms over his chest, his brow lifting a fraction. The businessman was back. "I want to see you again. Dating, but with no chains around either of our necks and no judgments about the way I do business. That's all I can offer."

But it wasn't enough. She loved him more than anything but he was no longer the man he'd been before that knock on their door. She glanced up at him. "Then I decline your offer, Mr. Tanner."

He glared at her with burning, reproachful eyes. "I have to be back in the office as early as possible."

She bit back her tears. She wasn't going to embarrass herself or give C. K. Tanner a scene to remember. "Then maybe you should go tonight. I'll explain to Jan and Frank that you had urgent business to get to."

"Is that what you want?" he ground out, coming to his feet.

She felt as if her whole life rested on this moment. "Why not? You got everything you came for."

A muscle twitched below his left eye as he stared down at her. Behind him the fire blazed. Abby held her breath, her heart curling up against the pain.

Finally he nodded, then stood. "I'll have the jet return for you in the morning."

"Don't bother," she said to his retreating frame. "I'll take a commercial flight."

He didn't say a word. A hot tear rolled down her cheek, and she wiped it away with the back of her hand. What had started out as the most wonderful day of her life was ending in ashes. She'd imagined them leaving this place together, strolling down by the lake, hand in hand. Not like this. Not like this, she silently repeated as she watched him quickly gather up his things and walk out the door.

Thunder rumbled outside.

She put her head in her hands and let the tears come.

Eleven

————

Tanner sat at his desk listening as rain poured from a gloomy sky and beat against the windows of his office like a thousand little drums. It was as though he was sitting in the heart of the storm and there was no sign of morning sunlight ahead.

His thoughts filtered back to a guest house by a lake and the red-haired beauty who had told him to leave so calmly it had made his insides twist. He'd missed her from the moment he'd walked out the door, but his pride, his control, his very sanity had warned him not to look back.

He'd had a miserable plane ride, without sleep and his mind on constant rewind—going over and over Abby's charges of duplicity and his two-word justification: "It's business."

He'd been at the office since four-thirty in the

morning, looking over paperwork, reading e-mails, waiting for the stock market to open on the East Coast—anything but look at those damned contracts.

He knew why he was miserable. He couldn't change and Abby didn't want to be with him the way he was. What he had to offer wasn't enough. But that didn't explain why the hell he felt so guilty about Swanson. Tanner's justification was a legitimate one. It was *just* business. It might be ruthless at times, but it was done every day in every country in the world.

He shook his head. That knowledge gave him no peace, only regret for the baser aspects of his profession.

For what seemed like the millionth time, Tanner read over Jeff's memo outlining the deal points he'd discussed with Harrison's people. It was a good deal, especially for Tanner Enterprises.

He leaned back in his chair and looked up at the ceiling as if it held answers. He'd spent the night thinking of options regarding Harrison, a way out— and only one made sense. And that one might just solve his problem and soothe his conscience while maintaining the ever-delicate and unwritten "good faith" rule that sound business relationships relied upon. That is, if he allowed himself to take it.

He knew that selling to Harrison could be justified in a hundred different ways: Jeff had taken the initiative without Tanner's knowledge, Swanson's deal didn't specify reselling restrictions, blah-blah-blah. But to present these deal points on Tanner Enterprises letterhead in the meeting at ten o'clock—actually moving this deal into the final stretch—that would be all him. And he felt no pride, no rush of adrenaline that usually accompanied this kind of coup, no satisfaction in having the upper hand.

He glanced at the clock on the wall: 9:30 a.m.

He cursed and rubbed at the stubble on his chin. He had to make a decision—Harrison would be arriving in half an hour. So what the hell was he waiting for?

A knock sounded at his door, reverberating off the light-gray walls. Who the hell was that? he grumbled to himself. It wouldn't be Jeff. He knew better than to provoke him today.

Damn, he didn't want to see anyone. Well, anyone but Abby.

"Come in," he growled.

The door opened slowly, and the first thing he saw was the mail cart. A broad smile came to his lips and a powerful relief filled him.

She was back at work where she belonged, where he could see her every day. His smile widened. Perhaps she'd even changed her mind about his—

"Good morning, sir." A short blonde he didn't recognize walked through the door and held a stack of mail out to him.

His smile faded. He gestured toward the wire basket. "Just put it in there. Thank you." Tomorrow. Abby would be back tomorrow. Why did that seem like months from now?

The young woman did as he asked, then looked at him, a question behind her eyes. "Should I put your mail here every day, sir?"

He shook his head. "Don't bother. Abby already knows the routine."

"Abby quit this morning, sir. I'll be your new mail—"

Tanner jackknifed to his feet. "What the hell do you mean, she quit?"

The girl backed up a few feet, her eyes wide. "Uh…she was in really early this morning. She said she had to quit, effective immediately."

"To go where? Do what?" He knew he was acting like a lunatic, not like the boss, but he didn't care. "Did she tell you where she was going?"

The girl shook her head. "She just said she got a better job."

Anger, helpless anger, surged through him. Better job with whom? And where? How could she just quit without talking to him first? What about her art and teaching? What about him?

What *about* him? he repeated silently. She wanted too much from him. Marriage, kids, commitment, ties that bind, a man who didn't screw over his friends in a quest to make money.

"Any outgoing mail, sir?"

Tanner looked up into the girl's expectant gaze, his gut twisting uncontrollably.

"No," he muttered. "Thank you. You can go."

He watched the girl turn and leave, his mind on others who had walked out with little care for what they'd left behind. But he couldn't blame his family this time. This time it was all him. He'd done the walking out, the running away. And for what? To save himself the pain that might never materialize?

Was he so scared of losing his heart that he wouldn't even try to open it?

His gaze flickered to the wire mesh basket, the very same one that Abby had knocked over the morning he'd asked her to be his wife. He couldn't help the pained chuckle that escaped his lips. She was so damned cute. The perfect combination of sweet and silly and sexy.

Suddenly his gaze caught on one of the envelopes in the basket. He narrowed his eyes, then grabbed it. He recognized that artistic scribble of his name. *Abby.* No stamp, no return address. Obviously, she'd dropped it off before she'd quit.

Pulse pounding in his ears, he tore open the envelope.

His chest tightened as the keys to the warehouse space he'd given her in trade for her part in their "marriage" dropped onto his desk. But his heart truly sank when his grandmother's ring fell directly onto the Harrison memo.

He leaned back in his chair, suddenly weary. In some hidden corner of his mind he realized he'd thought that if she were here, near him every day, maybe that would be enough—maybe there would still be a chance she would change her mind about his offer. Maybe she could look past the whole deal with Swanson.

He picked up the ring, rolled it between his thumb and forefinger as his mind traveled back again—to that day in Malibu when she'd let him slip his grandmother's ring on her finger, when she'd told him about her days as an artist's model, when they'd made ice-cream sundaes together in his kitchen.

Before he'd even really known her, he'd seen how amazing she was. Honest and willing to give anything to make a person happy. On first sight she'd loved the one sentimental, precious thing he had in the world: his grandmother's ring. His last tie to his family. But before she'd worn it, he'd never realized just how precious.

Oh, God, he loved her.

The realization assaulted him like an uppercut to the jaw.

He let the ring roll into his palm, and he made a fist around it.

Before Abby had worn his ring, before she was a part of his life, he was a different man. A person who, in truth, even he didn't like all that much. But she'd changed him. And now he couldn't see his life without her.

He glanced down at the ring on his own finger, his pulse pounding in his ears as it slowly dawned on him that he wanted to make a life with her, be committed to her, be bound to her by love and by promise.

But before he could offer his love to Abby—and pray that she still wanted it—he had to offer his honesty to the man who'd helped open his eyes to the truth.

Tanner glanced at the clock: 9:45 a.m.

He picked up the phone and dialed.

After several rings, he heard the voice he wanted to hear. "Swanson residence."

"Frank, it's Tanner."

"Everything all right, son? Abby said you had an emergency with a client."

Tanner took a deep breath. "She was covering for me, sir. I'd like to tell you the truth, starting with this—Abby and I aren't married."

"I know that."

Tanner's throat went dry. For the first time in his life he was rendered speechless.

"And I don't give a damn because I believe in you. Have from the start. Call it a sixth sense." Frank chuckled. "And hell, son, you can fix up that marriage business in an hour if you can find a justice of the peace."

I fell in love with you, Tanner. Or the man I thought you were. Her words echoed through his mind.

He gripped the phone, fighting to stay calm, in control, but he'd lost his head, his heart and he knew now he'd do anything to get her back. "Well, I'm not sure she'll have me now, Frank. I'm hoping you can help."

"Anything you need, son. Anything at all."

"Darn candy machines." Abby slammed her fist against the side of the machine, then waited to see if anything would happen.

Nothing did.

"Just my luck," she mumbled.

Her stomach growling, she turned away from the community center's ornery vending services and walked down the hallway. Break time was just about over, but she didn't feel like racing back to the room.

Tonight was her last class at the community center, and she still hadn't decided what to do about their future meeting place.

One thing she did know was that the building Tanner had offered her was not an option anymore. And it wasn't just her pride or what had happened between them. It was also the knowledge that they'd hurt Frank and Jan that made the idea of taking anything from Tanner impossible.

Except the memories of his deep-brown eyes, sexy smile and playful spirit. Or the feel of his mouth on hers, and the deep baritone that went soft and husky when he was making love to her.

Heat pooled low in her belly, and she wanted to kick herself. How was she going to get over him if she thought about things like that or the sweet, thoughtful way he'd made her confront her fear? Well, perhaps by remembering the fact that she couldn't do the same for him. He was knee-deep in past hurts and was determined to hold on to them. And no amount of love and kindness from her was going to help.

If only that knowledge could act as an antidote to Tanner, she thought miserably. The horrid truth was that no one had ever made her feel the way he did, and she knew no one ever would.

She stopped at the drinking fountain and let the cool water flow between her lips.

Just going into the office to resign yesterday had been so unbearable she'd spent the remainder of the day in bed with the covers over her head. But her mother's patchwork quilt had been no shelter. Her heart was broken, and the pieces were sharp and filled with wonderful memories that poked and stabbed at her constantly.

She'd thought of calling her mom or Dixie for a little support, but she just hated the thought of telling either one of them about the weekend, then explaining what an idiot she was for falling in love with the Playboy of the Western World. It was better for them to think she was happy, ready to start a new job. Even though she was miserable and sending out résumés.

Of course, she did have one solid job offer, although in her heart she knew she couldn't take it.

When Jan had driven her to the airport on Monday morning, the older woman had tactfully avoided questions about the state of Abby and Tanner's relationship. But she had offered Abby her friendship and a job—should she need one—with one of Frank's smallish companies doing art design and marketing. But the catch was she'd have to live in Minnesota. And though the idea of being miles away from Tanner appealed to her dispirited state of mind, she couldn't leave her family. Besides, when Jan and Frank found out about the fate of their company they wouldn't want to have anything to do with her.

Abby paused at the classroom door, giving her students a moment to finish their assignments. She couldn't help but smile halfheartedly as she recalled how they'd been full of compliments and hoots for her more sophisticated look, peppering her with questions like "Who's the lucky guy?" and "What did *you* do this weekend?"

Well, she just had to break out of this morose

mood, pretend to enjoy life until it became truth. Some of the students were going out for a drink after class. They'd always invited her to tag along. Maybe she'd go with them this time.

"All right, everybody," she began, moving to the front of the room. "Your assignment was to do a charcoal drawing of a body part. Yours or a friend's." She smiled at them. "And I remember saying to keep it artistic, not graphic."

Several groans filled the room, then laughter.

"I'm looking for details, shadows, distinctive markings." She clasped her hands together. "So keep working. I'm just going to walk around and take a look, offer some suggestions."

As Abby wound her way through the clusters of easels and chairs, she gave a compliment here, demonstrated a technique there, even held up a beautiful drawing of a shoulder for everyone to see.

"That tip is too blunt. Let me get you a pencil sharpener," she told one of her students as she headed toward the front of class, to her own personal supplies.

"Don't forget about me."

Abby whirled at the familiar voice, searching for its origin. But all she saw was the back of an easel. Her heart slamming against her ribs, she walked toward it and peered over the top.

Tanner smiled up at her. "I've taken every detail into account, Miss McGrady."

Abby gasped, grabbing on to the back of a chair for support. Tanner sat there, behind the easel, a charcoal pencil in his hand, a smile playing about his lips.

Bewildered, she could only ask, "What?"

"I did the assignment," he said simply.

"What are you doing here, Tanner?" Abby forced herself to stay calm, her voice low.

He shrugged. "Taking an art class. And it's Charles Kerry."

She felt her brow furrow.

"That's what the C. K. stands for."

Abby could only stare at him.

He smiled. "Charles Kerry Tanner. I was named after my father." The amused look suddenly left his eyes. "I've never told anyone that, Abby."

A dozen feelings rushed her from all sides. He was here in her class, sharing a confidence with her, smiling at her with hopeful eyes. Why? And why now? She took a stab in the dark. "I'm not coming back to work."

"That's not why I'm here." He gestured for her to come and stand beside him. "Aren't you going to look at my drawing, maybe offer some suggestions?"

She glanced around. The students were pretending to be working, but she knew they were all ears, waiting to see what would happen next. Lord, so was she. Just seeing him again made her heart hurt and her body ache for him. But she wasn't about to make a scene in front of the class.

Her throat tight, she walked around the easel and looked at his drawing. It was a quick sketch, clearly done by someone with little artistic training who had sneaked into her class on the break. But it had something, something his drawing of her from the other night had lacked. Warmth and character. Two hands were drawn side by side. One was small, female. The other was larger, more masculine and had a band around the fourth finger.

"It's fine," she said, making sure not to look directly at him.

"But something's missing, right?"

Her gaze flickered back to the drawing as he took his pencil and drew in a band on the fourth finger of the smaller hand. "That's better, don't you think?"

Finally she met his gaze. "I'm not sure it works. But we *do* tend to see things differently."

He took her hand in his. "Why don't we step outside and discuss it?"

"No," she said, jerking her hand away. "You came to my class. Whatever you have to say, you can just say it in front of everyone."

He stood up and cupped her face. "God, I miss kissing you, Abby."

She gasped, her cheeks burning. "Okay, let's go outside."

The class groaned as Abby took what felt like a five-mile walk to the door.

"Tell me why you're here," she demanded once they were out in the deserted hallway.

"Frank and I are going to be partners. We're going to run Swanson Sweets together. He really didn't want to retire, just wanted some of the burden taken off his shoulders." He smiled. "The Abby Apple is our first project. I wanted you to know."

"But...what about the deal?"

"I didn't do it. I couldn't do it. I sold Harrison one of Tanner Enterprise's most valuable subsidiaries instead—one he's wanted for a long time. I sold it for a song, by the way, but it was worth it.'' He shook his head. ''Because I almost made the biggest mistake of my life.''

Abby nodded stiffly. So he'd decided to do the right thing and he'd come to tell her about it. Why didn't that news fill her with sublime joy? ''It would've been a very big mistake. I'm glad you decided to work things out with Frank.''

He searched her gaze. ''I'm not talking about the company. I'm talking about you. I almost let you get away.'' He hauled her against him, brushing a kiss on her ear. ''I love you, Abby.''

The words hit her full force. She lifted her gaze to his. ''Say that again.''

''I love you. I love you so much,'' he said again softly, sweetly. ''All of my life, survival demanded that I learn how to hide my feelings and stay in control. I became a powerhouse in a business that thrived on ruthless, emotionless tactics.'' He released her just enough to take her face in his hands. ''I thought I was happy. But I was fooling myself. And I didn't realize it until you spilled coffee all over my desk, until you showed me that I could be a good businessman *and* an honorable man.''

His eyes darkened with emotion and passion and sincerity as he opened his soul to her. ''From the moment we met I felt like a kid, fighting to break free of the man I'd become. A man who was so convinced that love didn't exist he wouldn't risk his heart for anything or anyone. A man who knew that a woman like Abby McGrady would see straight through him if he did take that risk.''

"Who won?'' she asked quietly, sure of the answer but wanting to hear it from him.

"Well, I've got a convertible outside.'' He grinned like the confident devil he was. "You wanna go for a ride, park at the beach and neck for a couple hours?''

Abby laughed. "Then what?''

His eyes burned a savage fire. "Then you could marry me.''

"Oh, Tanner…'' She closed her eyes on her tears and felt one slide down her cheek. She couldn't form an answer, even though she had wanted to hear those words more than anything in the world.

He put his hand under her chin and lifted her gaze to his. "You love me?''

"Yes,'' she said breathlessly.

He kissed her hard, his lips claiming hers possessively, then he lowered to one knee. "Sweetheart, in front of all these people—''

"What people?''

Tanner gestured behind her. Abby glanced over her shoulder and saw her entire class peeking through the door, one interested, riveted face on top of another. She laughed as she turned back to face Tanner, but stopped when she saw he had the ring, that beautiful ring—his grandmother's ring—in his hand.

He smiled up at her. "I want promises and ties, a truckload of kids and a seat on the board of directors of the McGrady Art Center. I want to start over. I want a life. But most of all I want you.'' Her heart melted in the heat of his gaze. "I love you so much, Abby. Marry me?"

The silence was deafening. But inside Abby, bells and whistles were going off. She closed her eyes for just a moment, thanking God for answering her silent prayers. Tanner loved her, wanted her as much as she loved and wanted him.

She opened her eyes and smiled at him. "I will, Tanner. Yes, I do—"

He was on his feet in seconds, cutting her off with a hungry kiss as cheers and applause overcame the silence.

He released her long enough to slip the ring on her finger. "I think this belongs to you."

She slid her arms around his neck and held on tight. "I think this belongs to me, too."

He chuckled softly. "Forever, Mrs. Tanner."

"Forever," Abby repeated, knowing that nothing had ever sounded so sweet. But now that her husband was going to run a candy company, she thought as she melted against him, the possibilities were end-less….

*   *   *   *   *

New York Times bestselling author

LINDA HOWARD

tells an incredible story!

Readers have always clamored for Chance Mackenzie's
story. Now the brooding loner, welcomed into the
Mackenzie family but never quite at home, is on a
desperate assignment. He'll take any risk, tell any lie,
do whatever is necessary. But when fiery, independent
and yet vulnerable Sunny Miller becomes the one in
danger, can Chance take the final gamble?

Don't miss

A Game of Chance

Coming this September from Silhouette Books!

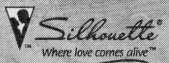

Silhouette® *Desire*®

presents

DYNASTIES: THE CONNELLYS

A brand-new miniseries about the Connellys of Chicago, a wealthy, powerful American family tied by blood to the royal family of the island kingdom of Altaria. They're wealthy, powerful and rocked by scandal, betrayal…and passion!

Look for a whole year of glamorous and utterly romantic tales in 2002:

January: **TALL, DARK & ROYAL by Leanne Banks**

February: **MATERNALLY YOURS by Kathie DeNosky**

March: **THE SHEIKH TAKES A BRIDE by Caroline Cross**

April: **THE SEAL'S SURRENDER by Maureen Child**

May: **PLAIN JANE & DOCTOR DAD by Kate Little**

June: **AND THE WINNER GETS…MARRIED! by Metsy Hingle**

July: **THE ROYAL & THE RUNAWAY BRIDE by Kathryn Jensen**

August: **HIS E-MAIL ORDER WIFE by Kristi Gold**

September: **THE SECRET BABY BOND by Cindy Gerard**

October: **CINDERELLA'S CONVENIENT HUSBAND by Katherine Garbera**

November: **EXPECTING…AND IN DANGER by Eileen Wilks**

December: **CHEROKEE MARRIAGE DARE by Sheri WhiteFeather**

Silhouette®
Where love comes alive™

If you enjoyed what you just read,
then we've got an offer you can't resist!

Take 2 bestselling
love stories FREE!
Plus get a FREE surprise gift!

Clip this page and mail it to Silhouette Reader Service™

IN U.S.A.
3010 Walden Ave.
P.O. Box 1867
Buffalo, N.Y. 14240-1867

IN CANADA
P.O. Box 609
Fort Erie, Ontario
L2A 5X3

YES! Please send me 2 free Silhouette Desire® novels and my free surprise gift. After receiving them, if I don't wish to receive anymore, I can return the shipping statement marked cancel. If I don't cancel, I will receive 6 brand-new novels every month, before they're available in stores! In the U.S.A., bill me at the bargain price of $3.57 plus 25¢ shipping and handling per book and applicable sales tax, if any*. In Canada, bill me at the bargain price of $4.24 plus 25¢ shipping and handling per book and applicable taxes**. That's the complete price and a savings of at least 10% off the cover prices—what a great deal! I understand that accepting the 2 free books and gift places me under no obligation ever to buy any books. I can always return a shipment and cancel at any time. Even if I never buy another book from Silhouette, the 2 free books and gift are mine to keep forever.

225 SDN DNUP
326 SDN DNUQ

Name	(PLEASE PRINT)	
Address	Apt.#	
City	State/Prov.	Zip/Postal Code

* Terms and prices subject to change without notice. Sales tax applicable in N.Y.
** Canadian residents will be charged applicable provincial taxes and GST.
All orders subject to approval. Offer limited to one per household and not valid to current Silhouette Desire® subscribers.
® are registered trademarks of Harlequin Books S.A., used under license.

DES02   ©1998 Harlequin Enterprises Limited

magazine

♥———————————————————————— **quizzes**

Is he the one? What kind of lover are you? Visit the **Quizzes** area to find out!

♥——————————————— **recipes for romance**

Get scrumptious meal ideas with our **Recipes for Romance**.

♥————————————————— **romantic movies**

Peek at the **Romantic Movies** area to find Top 10 Flicks about First Love, ten Supersexy Movies, and more.

♥————————————————————— **royal romance**

Get the latest scoop on your favorite royals in **Royal Romance**.

♥——————————————————————————— **games**

Check out the **Games** pages to find a ton of interactive romantic fun!

♥————————————————— **romantic travel**

In need of a romantic rendezvous? Visit the **Romantic Travel** section for articles and guides.

♥————————————————————— **lovescopes**

Are you two compatible? Click your way to the **Lovescopes** area to find out now!

where love comes alive—online...

SINTMAG